MCC

2(.

MW01612251

POST EXODUS

Robert Christiansen

Jordan,
keep your wheels
moving down the
road.

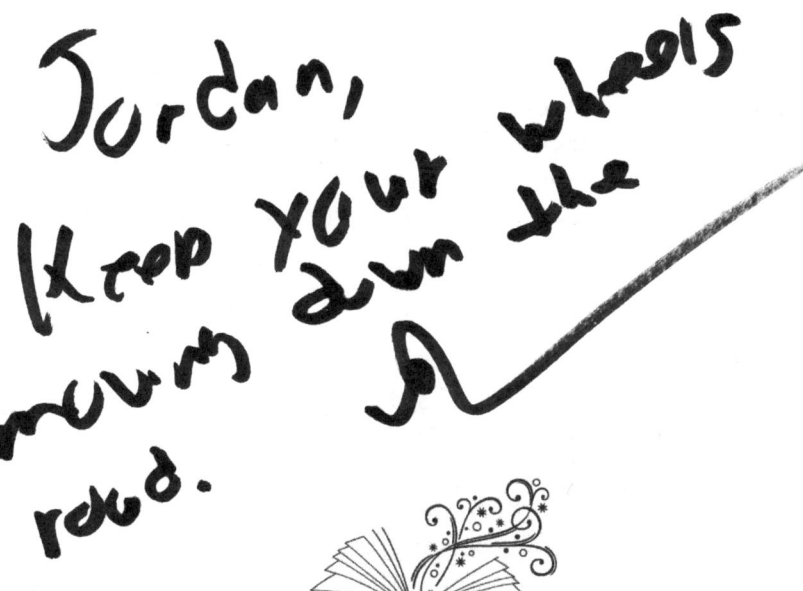

Amazing Things Press

Book design by Julie L. Casey

This book is a work of fiction. Any names, characters, or
incidents are the product of the author's imagination and
are used fictitiously. Any resemblance to actual events,
locales, or persons, living or dead is purely coincidental.

ISBN 978-0692546888
Printed in the United States of America.

For more information, visit
www.amazingthingspress.com

PROLOGUE

Excerpts from media reports during and after construction of the Arks

"Scientists from many disciplines all over the world are predicting a tragedy that would mean the end to all humanity and a total end to all life on Earth. Numerous astronomers have sighted a large meteor on a collision course with Earth..."

"Engineers from NASA, ESA, the Russian Space Agency, and CNSA have come together to cooperatively design large ships, collectively called the Arks, that could carry millions of people safely into deep space..."

"Protesters around the world have started demonstrations in countries that do not have their own space agencies or launch facilities. They are expressing concerns about their respective cultures being forgotten due to a lack of representation on the Arks."

"A fleet of cargo ships carrying supplies and equipment arrived in the port of Ras al Khafji today. The shipments were made in order to build launch facilities in the Middle East. The International Ark Organization has stated they are doing this for two reasons. The first is to ferry laborers to the orbital construction platforms where the Arks are being built. The second reason is a show of appreciation for the drastic lowering of petroleum prices during this time of global crisis."

"Protests have all but ceased as people from countries around the globe begin to move themselves into their cabins on the Arks. The only vocal group still clamoring to be heard is insisting that no human beings be left behind on Earth. They strongly feel that those who wish to stay be removed from their homes by force. A military General stated, on the record, that he would forcibly move those folks on the condition that the protesters give up their spaces on the Arks to make room. No response to this statement from the protesters has yet been made..."

"Cheers could be heard around the world today at 7:00 am Greenwich Mean Time as the engines of all the Arks were simultaneously engaged. While there is still some work to be completed before launch, the engines now make the Arks self sufficient and significantly closer to being ready for launch."

"Welcome from the inaugural broadcast of the ArkNet, a news and information channel for the residents and crews of the Arks. The final Ark, named Argos, boarded the last of its resident passengers and sealed the outer doors to the living quarters just yesterday..."

"The first Ark to be officially completed, affectionately dubbed Noah, passed its final checks and has been certified as spaceworthy..."

"We are entering the final month of ArkNet. As the Arks continue to head out on their respective courses, the distances between them will continue to grow and require too much energy to maintain constant contact between us all. Before we start our farewells, there is a remarkable greeting that needs to be extended. The first confirmed child conceived on the Arks was born this morning. Rick and Julia Johnson of the Enterprise welcomed their son Kirk to our journey..."

First Delivery

I finally had a destination and path for my new life. It was a good feeling.

A long stretch of empty roads reached out to the horizon before me. The sound of my bicycle's tires on the very worn pavement provided a gentle counterpoint to the wind rushing against my ears. The gentle slope of the hill required me to occasionally pump the pedals to keep up my speed. Even though the sun had risen many minutes before, it had yet to make an appearance above the trees lining each side of the road. While some might use the peaceful time to ponder their lives or philosophize existence itself, I simply shut my mind down and let my body do what it wished.

My peaceful ride was more than just a relaxing getaway, however. I had a purpose and a mission. I wore my vest at all times. An unofficial mark of my informal position as a messenger. The obvious pockets contained letters and notes destined for the residents of the towns along my route. A small metal box rested comfortably in a hidden pocket inside of my vest.

The box was to be delivered at the furthest point of my journey, a small town surviving around a defunct industrial park on the West Coast. That was many hundreds of miles and months ahead of me. For now, though, there was simply me, the road, the trees, and the sun peeking its way between the leaves dangling from the top limbs.

My name is Cade Van Housen and I'm a messenger. I decided to travel the largely empty country and carry important packages, messages, and letters from town to town in exchange for home-cooked meals or supplies for the journey. For as long as I am able, I will travel the land from coast to coast, in every direction of the compass, to bring news and information to those in my path.

I was raised in a small town on the East Coast in the former state of Massachusetts. With populations spread so thin, state borders were meaningless except as navigation aids. Maps hadn't been redrawn since the Exodus. There was no reason to redefine useless borders and not enough people to warrant recreating imaginary lines.

More than fifty years ago a global tragedy was predicted, a meteor that would destroy the earth. Countries came together and built giant ships in order to evacuate the planet. National borders meant nothing as laborers collectively gathered materials and assembled the components of giant Arks to carry humankind across the stars to safety. It was a glorious time as peoples of different countries, races, and religions came together as one species with a common goal for all. Billions of people boarded the Arks when they were completed. Access to the ships was given with no regard to race, nationality, or religion. Seeds of plants and DNA samples of other species were stored in the hopes of saving more than just humanity if a new planetary home could be found. The fleet of ships departed in separate directions with plenty of time remaining before the predicted tragedy was to strike.

However, not everyone escaped on the Arks. Some people chose to stay behind and perish with their ancestral home. Those that lived in remote areas or preferred to exist in isolation weren't forced to join everyone else on the Arks. Others were deemed undesirable and intentionally left behind. The criminally insane and particularly violent would be set free after the Arks were sealed for departure. Those that would simply not survive a prolonged journey due to extreme age or illness were made as comfortable as possible. The caretakers of the weak and ill remaining behind were given a choice, many choosing to stay and tend to the patients they had been responsible for. Those that were able celebrated all over the world the day the Arks departed on their combined mission of preventing the lives that had begun on Earth from being wiped completely out of existence.

The predicted date of the apocalypse finally came. The handful of remaining human residents on Earth had prepared themselves for their life to end. Some got extremely intoxicated. Quite a few chose to honor the end of their existences with more intimate activities. They gathered in pairs, trios, and larger groupings in order to spend their last hours in pleasure and ecstasy. Consequences were never a consideration since there would be no time for hangovers, brain damage, or any other ill effects of their actions.

Nobody had expected what happened next. Absolutely nothing. There was no meteoric impact that led to a shock wave circling the globe, shattering structures and obliterating life. Plants continued to wave in the gentle breezes. Wildlife kept up its habits of strolling through life and surviving the "eat or be eaten" existence. The small number of humans that hadn't departed with the Arks suddenly found themselves able to make long-term plans. The shock caused some to take their own lives, further decreasing the extremely low number of people on Earth. Others decided to celebrate their continued existence by rediscovering love and starting families. Once again, there was a slow growth in the human population on Earth.

Which brought me to my new profession:

long-distance messenger.

The previous day, I had walked into the main square of town from my family's farmlands. It was a walk I had done frequently in the past, but this was the first time I was doing it without food to sell at the community market. I checked the message boards in the center of the town square for a letter intended for a recipient far away. The furthest destination I could see was a small town south of Dallas. It would mean a very long walk, but I could make a few stops along the way. Maybe take a letter to Memphis and another to a new village near the former border between Oklahoma and Texas.

I was about to grab the message to Dallas when I sensed someone behind me. "You don't want to go there. Traveling on foot, you will get there in the middle of summer. Way too hot to be walking by yourself."

I turned around to look at the man that was talking to me. I had seen him around town before, but I wasn't sure exactly who he was. When he bought food, he bought enough for many people. Rumors mentioned by others in the market were that he worked with a handful of people at some advanced lab outside of town. Nobody knew what the lab made or studied, but everyone knew it existed. Some of the older town citizens said the building had been a government-run facility before the Exodus and was emptied just after. In recent years, the lab had become active again. There was no government anymore to provide funding for the research done there. There was nobody to oversee or regulate what happened there either.

"Do you have something for me to take elsewhere? I would be more than happy to deliver it for you."

"I do have something that needs to be delivered. However, it's not a letter or note that would be up on this message board. It's a box. A sealed metal box. The contents need to be delivered to a lab near Redding, California. You won't be able to open the box. I will email the director of the other lab to let him know you are coming and how to open the box."

I was willing to accept his offer and was absorbing the rest of what he was saying until one word caught my attention. "Did you say you would email the other lab? Do you actually have the Internet in that old lab out there?"

"We do have Internet. It's not like what was around before the Exodus, but a very few of us can still communicate between ourselves. Many of the servers of the old network are no longer functioning, but enough still are that we can exchange brief messages."

"I understand. I'll take your package to Redding, but it'll take a long time for me to walk there. If your item has any kind of deadline, I can't guarantee it will arrive on time."

The man reached into a backpack and pulled out a small metal box with a complicated latch on it. It was a little bit smaller than my mother's jewelry box. The box was silver and shiny. The metal looked new as opposed to the recycled metal containers I usually saw. "There is no deadline for the package's delivery, but I will give you something as payment to speed you along."

I put the box in one of the inside pockets of my vest and followed the gentleman down a side street. We walked into a neighborhood filled with large, empty houses that had overgrown lawns and dying trees. Nobody lived in this part of town and people rarely visited here. I had no reason to suspect this guy's intentions, but I felt a little nervous anyway. He led me into the back-yard of one of the vacant homes. There was a path cleared through the tall grass and weeds from the fence to a small shed. The man opened the shed with a key and stood aside. Small flecks of dust floated in spotlights of sun in the nearly empty storage shed. The sole item inside was a bicycle that looked brand new.

I looked at the gentleman and back into the shed. I noticed him nod at me and I entered the shed to retrieve the bike. I gave it a good look as I rolled it into the sunlight. It was silver, the metal very similar to the box stashed in my pocket. A pair of large black saddlebags strad- dled the back tire. Each bag was large enough to fit all of my possessions. There was a pair of empty holsters on each side of the front tire. One was sized for a handgun; the other could fit a shotgun or rifle. The tires had all-terrain treads and were very thick. It would take a serious ef- fort to puncture a hole in one of them. The chain and front and rear derailleurs were protected by a lightweight cover that could be popped off easily for maintenance. Barring any significant tragedy, this was a bicycle that would probably outlive me.

My benefactor watched me inspect the bike closely before speaking again. "The outer pocket of the right saddlebag has all the maps you should need. The saddlebag itself contains a va- riety of dried fruits and some meat jerky along with enough water for about three days. I'm sure you can pick up more supplies along your way to get yourself to Redding. Like I said, there is no specific deadline. We do need that package de- livered as soon as you can though."

"I promise I'll do my best to get to Redding as quickly as I can and on the most direct route possible. I swear this on my life and the souls of family members that have passed on." This was the most sincere oath I could give. In the current times, family and life was all that anyone could truly have.

"When you get there, just tell them the box is from Eastern Eddie. They will know exactly what you mean and what is in there."

I nodded my understanding and walked my new bike out of the weedy yard. I rode it a ways then stopped and took out the maps that were in the saddlebag pocket, spread them out on a stone picnic table, and began to study them in order to find a route to Redding, California. There were a couple of large regional maps with major highways and interstates clearly marked on them. There were also a lot of smaller local maps that showed roads through towns. There were so many routes I could choose from; I would let any messages that needed to be carried on the way dictate the exact details of my path.

The first leg of my journey proved to be easy and peaceful, but of course, that couldn't last for long.

POST EXODUS

The rest of the day passed in the same gentle way. As evening approached, I realized it was time to find myself something to eat for dinner. The fact I hadn't seen a town for a couple of days meant that hunting should be easy enough and provide me with a decent meal. I knew that if I could catch some prey quickly enough, I would be able to cook all the meat overnight over a fire to preserve it for snacking while on the road.

I carried two weapons on my bike. A shotgun hung in a holster just behind my seat next to the saddlebags that straddled the rear tire so as to blend in with them. I had practiced drawing it both subtly and quickly many times. I wanted to be as prepared as possible should I find someone that wanted to be less than helpful. However, I didn't use the shotgun for hunting. Ammunition was too difficult to acquire to waste. For capturing food I used a longbow. Arrows were cheap to replace and could be used a number of times before a new one was required.

I removed the bow from its holder along the cross beam of my bike. A careful inspection revealed no flaws or excessive wear on the bow or the string. Slinging the quiver across my back, I walked my bike into some low bushes along the road to hide it from view. I mentally marked the location before moving deeper into the trees. My footsteps were careful and intentional. So few vehicles traveled the roads since the Exodus, it was not unusual to see deer or other animals lurking on or alongside highways that were once heavily traveled.

Not far into the forest, I spied a clear running stream. A perfect place to spot animals coming for a drink. The low brush between the trees showed signs of a number of animal trails leading to the area. Apparently it was a popular place to slake their thirst. I hoped I wouldn't have to wait long for my potential dinner to appear. I nocked an arrow on the taut bowstring. Settling comfortably against a tree, I kept my eyes on the stream and my ears wide open.

My wait wasn't long at all. Just over an hour later, a deer carefully stepped out from between a couple of trees. I raised my bow and pulled back the string, even though the deer's body was still being blocked from a clear shot by some small brush. The deer would be completely visible when it moved forward to take a drink. I slowly and silently rose, keeping my back against the tree as I sighted where the deer would be along the shaft of my arrow. I knew that any second now the animal would move into position and I would have myself a fresh meal and meat for days.

Then a noise behind and to the left of me caused every living being in the whole area to freeze. Something else in the brush had moved. Something not particularly careful. This eliminated the possibility of it being a four-legged predator. It could only be a two-legged hunter, and an inept one at that.

The deer turned and ran the other way. Before it had even finished its turn, I had spun my body towards the source of the sound that had ruined my night. With my bow fully drawn and my arrow ready to fly, I stared at a ragged looking man. He had a bushy beard that was as unkempt as his clothes. His hair reached down past his shoulders and looked like it had been washed only slightly more recently than it had been cut. The hair on his face and the wear and tear on his skin made estimating his age almost impossible. He wore a camouflage jacket over a dirty brown shirt and black denim pants. All of this was the second thing I noticed. The first thing to catch my eye was the rifle pointed in my direction.

I took a second to cool the anger that had been building inside me before speaking to the man that cost me my meal. "You just allowed a few days worth of good meat to run away. Explain yourself before I put another hole in that shirt of yours."

His voice was deep and strong. "You come hunting on my property and dare to threaten me? Who is it you seem to think you are?"

"What do you mean by calling this your property? There were no markers or indicators. I saw no homes anywhere near here. Obviously the land isn't being farmed. As for me, I'm a messenger. I have no home, no family with me, and no allegiances with any group. I simply travel around delivering notes, letters, and information in any way I can. Why don't you lower your gun and we'll talk about what kind of claim you think you have."

"Me lower my gun? That is real funny. You're the one with that wimpy little stick with some string on it. Put your toy down and walk out of my forest before I put so much lead in you that you'll never be able to pass a metal detector again."

"You may call my bow a toy, but it can put a hole cleanly through any one of your body parts I choose. What you don't seem to realize is that time isn't on your side. The longer we stand here aiming at each other, the lower your chances of survival."

"And what exactly makes you think that?"

"As we stand here your arms will get tired. Your weapon will lower and throw your aim off. The longer we're here, the more likely you are to wound me somewhere unimportant or miss me completely. I, on the other hand, have another issue in this standoff. As my arms tire my aim remains true, but the bowstring is more likely to slip from my weakening grip. The sooner you lower your gun, the less likely you are to have an arrow shaft sticking out of your chest."

The guy seemed to consider the situation carefully. I gave the string a slight twitch to hurry his thought processes. After a few seconds that seemed to stretch into an hour at least, he lowered his rifle. I relaxed the tension on my bowstring as I lowered the bow. We now looked at each other across the bushes in a slightly less tense manner.

As my body relaxed and the adrenaline of the hunt and standoff drained from my bloodstream, I asked the stranger a simple question. "You managed to scare off the only source of protein in the area. What are you going to do to replace it?"

"My first instinct is to let you walk away alive in exchange for chasing off your dinner. However, some things seem to have changed in the world and I need information. If you come with me, I will feed you and you can explain to me why I can't seem to get any kind of communication signals."

I was reluctant to accept his offer. Then curiosity got the better of me. What kind of signals was he expecting to receive? There hadn't been any kind of regular broadcasts since before I was born. Radio and television stations weren't exactly a high priority when most villages and towns were small enough that important information could be spread to everyone by a note in the village center or simple word of mouth. There was an occasional shortwave signal now and then, but these tended to be very brief messages reaching a rather short range.

As a show of faith, I placed my arrow back in its quiver and unstrung my bow. "I will accept a meal in exchange for whatever information I can provide. You can decide if what I have to say is worth more and compensate me however you see fit."

"Follow me," he said simply as he removed the clip from his rifle and ejected the single round from the chamber. Most people would have caught the unused round to save and reload later. This guy let the complete bullet fall to the grass at his feet. I wondered how large of a supply he had to allow this valuable piece of ammunition to go to waste.

We walked toward the stream in a route that was clearly different than the one he had used to get behind me. Reaching the banks of the flowing water, we moved downstream to a pool I hadn't noticed earlier. Next to the pool was a tall pile of rocks. The guy strolled up to the pile and placed his hand on a slab slightly bigger than the mattress on the bed my parents slept in when I was growing up.

He raised the slab of stone as though it weighed nothing at all. Behind it was a cave that sloped down steeply under the pile of rocks. Stairs were carved into the floor to make descending easier and safer.

"Please, you first." He gestured me in before him. I stepped forward and proceeded down the steps into the darkness below. The only light was from the open doorway behind me. The guy's shadow blocked this light as he moved inside the doorway himself. I stopped as the light disappeared completely with the closing of the stone slab door.

The darkness didn't last long. At almost the same instant as I heard the door thunk closed there was also the faint click of a metal latch. That click was quickly followed by the hum of electricity as the tunnel was suddenly filled with light from a string of bulbs hanging from the roof. "It's a safety feature. The lights will only come on once the door is closed and latched. No chance of their glow accidentally revealing the door's existence."

I could now see the bottom of the stairs a few feet below me. The tunnel extended further forward from the bottom step. Where I expected a rough stone floor, there was a smooth concrete pad instead. If there were a house above us instead of just forest, then we would be walking down to its basement. Apparently this man wanted or needed to live in a place that was well hidden from others.

I was surprised at what was before me as I reached the bottom of the steps. Instead of a musty basement, there was a large living space. It suddenly occurred to me that I was in one of the survival bunkers my parents had talked about. Some people had built them during and after the Exodus. They had hoped to survive the Tragedy-That-Wasn't by placing a thick layer of earth over their heads. It was both unnecessary and futile. If the meteor had struck Earth, it would have been easier for the planetary population to hide underground than it was to build the ships and launch them if that would have been a solution to the global event.

I stopped just inside the opening between the stairs and the shelter's expansive interior. The resident of this homey hole in the ground finally introduced himself as he stepped by me and entered his abode. "My name is Kevin. Welcome to my home. Please make yourself comfortable and I will get some food warming up for us."

I moved to the soft chairs Kevin gestured towards as he walked to a side chamber lined with shelves. A convenient pantry was carved out of the stone wall. Kevin picked up a handful of tins from the shelves and carried them to a counter in the area that was obviously the kitchen. He began preparing a meal for us while telling me about himself.

"My parents moved us down here a couple days before the planet was supposed to be wiped out. I was less than a year old at the time. My entire life has been spent down here. Most of what we needed came from recycling or nonperishable food like I'm making now. Power comes from a combination of solar cells hidden in the trees and a submerged water wheel in that stream we walked along.

"Life was good with my parents and me. They educated me and gave me the knowledge I needed to survive. A few months ago things changed. My parents passed away. I don't have enough medical skills to determine if it was a disease or simply old age. After a short time I began to feel lonely. I powered up the various radios we have so I could try to find someone else to talk to. When I was unable to pick up any kind of signal, I decided to wander above and see if I could finally contact another person."

He finished speaking and cooking at about the same time. The plate he placed in front of me wasn't particularly full, but it did have more variety than I usually ate in one meal. Potatoes and some kind of meat covered in sauce. Green beans warm and soft without being too limp. Kevin and

I each took a few bites in silence, only the sounds of our utensils on our plates echoing in the subterranean home. Catching him looking at me, I figured I should share the information with him that was to be my payment for this meal.

I told him what little I knew of the time before the Exodus. Since the great tragedy had been avoided five decades before, and I was just twenty years old myself, I couldn't explain much to him. The reason he wasn't able to pick up any broadcast signals wasn't due to any damage to the technology or a lack of power to the stations. It was the simple matter of a lack of anyone with the free time or desire to run the stations.

After digesting dinner and the information I had given him, Kevin leaned back in his chair. "I thank you for letting me know how things are in the outside world. It may be some time before I decide to leave my home for any extended period, but I do desire more human contact. I do have one more offer for you. It will be dark soon, too dark for you to safely return to your journey. I will let you rest here for the night if you tell me why you travel as a messenger."

"I left home for one simple reason. There wasn't enough space for me. I am the youngest of five children. My three older brothers each were given a portion of the land my parents own to handle how they want. My sister, the oldest amongst us, moved onto land owned by her husband's parents. If I had remained home, the land would have been equally divided between my brothers and me. By leaving, my brothers each get a larger tract of land. In exchange, I received whatever supplies and equipment my brothers could give me to start my journey with. Besides, I have no real desire to settle down and spend the rest of my life farming."

"Makes sense to me." Kevin seemed satisfied with my story. He got up and started to clear the dirty dishes from the table. I interrupted his activity and started to take the plates and utensils to the sink myself. As I washed them with running water from the sink, Kevin got a sleeping bag, a pillow, and an extra blanket for me. I laid the sleeping bag on the floor and crawled into it. There was no reason to expect it to get cold enough to need the blanket, but I kept it nearby in case the temperature inside this underground home happened to drop.

Kevin turned off the majority of the lights, leaving the room in near darkness. Only a few isolated bulbs remained on. I was sure it was for my safety if I wandered in the night. Kevin could probably walk the entire place in pitch-blackness and never even stub a toe. Despite the darkness, I had trouble falling asleep. It was too quiet in this deep, safe home. I had become quite accustomed to the sounds of wind shuffling through leaves and small animals moving amongst the brush.

The only sound here was the very soft movement of air through a ventilation system. I shifted and rolled restlessly for a time before the long day's ride and my full belly combined to carry me to dreamland.

I was wakened the next morning by Kevin's movements in another room as he prepared for the day. He decided he would go back east to check on a family house his parents had told him about. They had assumed it was destroyed while they hunkered down here. The home was near a good-sized town that sounded like the one I passed through recently. In the meantime, I would continue west. I had slept in my clothes, removing only my vest and placing it under my pillow. I extracted myself from the sleeping bag and rolled it up. While Kevin finished his preparations, I studied the road map I kept in my vest pocket. I had exchanged notes with other messengers regarding roads still accessible and areas controlled by violent groups that should be avoided. The map in my hand only covered the local area. I had more maps in the saddlebags of my bicycle, all kept up to date from information exchanged with other messengers.

Kevin and I said our farewells at the rocky entrance to his home. He showed me the hidden release to the door should I ever need to return here and he wasn't around. The door was a wooden panel disguised to look like a stone slab.

Without triggering the hidden release from the outside, a potential intruder would find the door as difficult to move as the large stone slab it resembled. A brief walk led me back to my bike. It had remained untouched the entire night. A quick snack of some dried jerky and a sip of water from my stream-filled canteen made for a light breakfast before I returned to my ride. I didn't boost my supplies like I had expected, but there would be many more chances in the future.

THE CAGE

I was traveling a route that had me hopping back and forth across the border between the former states of Ohio, Kentucky, and Indiana. This area was heavily traveled. Many of the towns and villages here had facilities for visiting guests with destinations elsewhere. More than one had the modern version of a hotel, an empty house with multiple bedrooms kept clean by neighbors. Someone passing through could simply walk in the front door and pick themselves a room to sleep in. A particularly friendly neighbor may also have a sign in their window stating meals available for visiting travelers. Places like this were favorites of messengers everywhere.

I was approaching one such town and ready for a rest. I had been pushing myself hard for the last three days with an urgent message for one of the leaders of this town. There was no single mayor or leader here but, instead, a council that led the entire town. The message I was carrying was for an influential member of this council. Because my bicycle allowed me more speed than simply walking, I had made it to the town two days before the deadline the sender had given me. Now I only had to find the council member and make the delivery. Most messages could be left in slots of message boards that were publicly accessible. I was emphatically instructed to put this particular message in the gentleman's hands directly. The message board would be near the center of town and hopefully, the council's offices would be as well.

I came around a curve in the road and saw the town coming into view amongst the trees. It was a classic town that had centuries of history. Tall church spires rose above the slanted roofs of homes and businesses alike. Only one thing looked out of place. On the far edge of town was a large gray brick building. It was square and taller than even the crosses on top of the church bell towers. I couldn't quite put my finger on it, but something about the building gave me the impression it was built after the Exodus.

As I entered the town, I was greeted by an armed guard. He flagged me down while keeping his rifle aimed at the ground. It made me a little nervous but not threatened enough to draw my shotgun. I rode up to him and stopped, straddling my bike as he greeted me in a mechanical manner with a well practiced speech.

"Welcome to the town of Greenville. We have a block of homes for visitors just east of the town center. Many of the neighbors open their doors to serve meals to guests. Please enjoy yourself and obey our local laws and regulations."

"Thank you, sir. I have a message for Johan of the City Council. Do you know where I might find him?"

The guard pondered my request for a few seconds. I couldn't tell if he was sizing me up to see if he could trust me, thinking about the answer to my question, or was surprised by being addressed directly. He eventually gave me basic directions to the building that housed the city council's offices where Johan could most likely be found. I thanked him and started pedaling into the town of Greenville.

The guard's directions led me to the City Council's building quickly enough. It was a typical building in the commercial district of the town. The main difference, besides most of the other buildings being empty, were the words "Council Offices" in bold letters above the door. I entered and found the first room comfortable and slightly crowded. There were enough people scattered around the room that I couldn't see much of the décor or the walls themselves. The folks in the room all seemed to know each other well and were chatting in a friendly manner. It didn't appear as though any of them had urgent business with the council. Some were sipping what appeared to be coffee from thick mugs;

others had small cups of water. One man sitting in the corner appeared to be nearly asleep despite the level of noise from all the simultaneous conversations. Everyone was so involved in what they were doing, no one even noticed my entrance. I loudly cleared my throat and slammed the door shut behind me. This caused everyone in the entire room to fall silent, as though someone had flipped a switch to turn them off. All eyes, even the ones of the gentleman in the corner, snapped around to look at me.

"I have an important message here for Johan, a member of the Greenville City Council. Would one of you happen to be him or can you direct me to where he is at the moment?"

A gentle whisper wandered through the room before silence regained its claim over everyone. Then the sleepy man in the corner piped up. "Yo, Joe! Get your ass out here. Got a special delivery for you."

A rather large individual emerged from a door I hadn't seen through the crowd. As he passed through the lobby area, the others stepped out of his way. The people parted before him and then closed immediately after he passed. The space created around him rippled through the crowd like a trout swimming upstream. He didn't have to do anything to make folks get out of his way, they just naturally sensed him and moved when he got close enough and moved back after he passed. This maneuver had either been practiced often or occurred frequently enough to become habit. The motion of the group stopped when the man I assumed to be Johan reached me.

His voice was deep and gravely. It certainly fit a man of his height and muscular build. "So you have a message for me, little man? Hand it over." He extended his hand and held it patiently, waiting for the envelope.

"I was given a phrase to ask before handing over the message. You are to answer a question a certain way. What colors are the owl's eyes?"

The large man just stared at me and didn't say another word. While we had been chatting, the older man that was resting in the corner had quietly made his way so he was standing next to me unnoticed. He spoke in a tone that commanded respect and could get a snake to stand at attention and salute. I straightened my spine a little as he spoke the phrase I had been told only Johan would know. "The owl's eyes are the colors of intelligence and wisdom."

I tore my eyes off the large man and refocused my attention to Johan. My hand reached into a side pocket of my vest and extracted the sole envelope that was there. I held the envelope out to the smaller man before me. His gaze traveled up and down me slowly as he fully took in my presence there. He grabbed the envelope and tore it open in a movement so fast it reminded me of the strike of a snake. His eyes moved back and forth as he read the note and a smile started to stretch across his lightly wrinkled face. As he looked up from the paper, I saw the smile on Johan's lips didn't reach his eyes. He quickly started barking orders around the room.

"Jack and Thomas, get the nets ready. We have a caravan coming through in just over a week. Angus, double-check the levels in the extra water casks. Joe, get some lumber and prepare some fencing for containment. Steve, Lucy, and Greg, go to the orchards and pick some fruits. Brandon and Slick, get to the community vegetable gardens and harvest anything ripe. Jem and Eric, get the fires going in the kitchen and get some pots and pans out. This is going to be a good-sized group so we will need lots of extra food for them. The rest of you need to get to the Cage and closely inspect all the equipment there. Make sure it's clean and in good condition. We don't need anything breaking like it did last time we had this many folks in at once."

The room quickly emptied as everyone got to work. Only two people remained besides me and the mysterious Johan. They were cleaning up the mess left behind by everyone's hasty departure. Coffee mugs and water cups were collected and carried to another room. Chairs and tables that had been moved were returned to their places in the middle of the room. Johan glanced around to make sure everyone had left before turning his attention back to me.

"Thank you for getting this message to us so quickly. I realize how hard you must have driven yourself to get here ahead of the deadline. If you have some time, would you like to rest in our town for the remainder of the day? You can enjoy a show tonight and get back on the road tomorrow."

"You are very welcome. I would appreciate a good day's rest. I also look forward to enjoying some company this evening."

Johan gave me some directions to a visitor's neighborhood where I could find a vacant house to rest in. He promised to meet me before sunset and escort me to the promised evening show.

The house was a much nicer one than some I had seen so far. It was two stories tall with all the bedrooms on the second floor. In the well-stocked kitchen, I was a little surprised to find a refrigerator that was still humming. Most towns fortunate enough to have electricity used it for permanent residents, never for the comforts of someone just passing through. The residents of this town seemed to be doing very well for themselves. If the rest of the city's leading council was anything like Johan, their leadership skills must be considerable in order to elevate the town as much as they had.

I had ridden so much the last few days and

slept very little in order to complete the rush delivery. I sat on a downstairs couch for a minute to rest before making the climb up the stairs to collapse in one of the bedrooms. I never made it off the couch. As I fell asleep, my mind started wandering around the odd gray, block building I had first spotted when I came into town. My subconscious insisted on making it into something evil and full of horrors. I refused to believe a sweet and helpful town like Greenville could ever tolerate something as inhumane as the images my mind was coming up with.

I was awoken by a knocking on the front door. Rising from the comfortable couch, I groggily walked over to see who the visitor was. As I passed a window, I realized the light coming through was different than it had been when I first sat down. I had napped for a few hours and Johan was knocking on the door to escort me to the evening's entertainment. I wasn't sure what to expect as far as transportation for us. Walking was the most likely option, but the two of us riding bicycles there together was possible. I had even seen some people travel through towns together in carts drawn by horses. I was in no way prepared for what was on the street behind Johan as I opened the door.

An actual automobile was parked in the street. It hadn't been there before so I knew it wasn't one of the abandoned empties that lined some of the less used highways and streets. This was a functional, four-wheeled, mobile mode of transportation. This particular model only had two seats and no room for storage. I could hear no engine rumbling so it was either off to conserve fuel or had a power source other than an internal combustion engine.

Johan simply grinned at my look of surprise and slight amazement at the realization of what was before me. "It's a real car alright. Runs off of electric batteries. They are recharged by the solar cells on the back window or by being plugged into a special electrical socket back at the council office. There is more than enough juice in them to get us where we need to go tonight. Do you want to freshen up, or are you ready to go now?"

I looked over my clothes quickly. They were slightly rumpled from being worn while I slept on the couch, but nothing that couldn't be fixed with a quick brushing with my hands. However, I had been wearing them for the three days I had been hurrying to make this delivery. There were no obvious marks or stains on my shirt, but a noticeable stink would be rising from me soon. "It's been a couple days since my last shower. If it would be less offensive, I could shower first. Otherwise, we can go now."

"Given how quickly you traveled to get here on time, I imagine a shower would feel good. Go right ahead and take as long as you wish. It's down that hallway on the right, second door on the left. The first door is a closet that is stocked with some clean clothes in a variety of sizes. Feel free to grab anything that fits."

This town rose higher and higher in my estimation. To offer showers so readily and have closets stocked with extra clothes was nearly unheard of. The vast majority of items were taken along on the Arks during the Exodus. What was left was claimed by those that stayed behind and used or recycled into other useful items. This town was so welcoming to visitors, I was surprised it wasn't full of those who decided to stay and enjoy the hospitality even longer.

I entered the simple bathroom. It had a small shower in the corner with a sink and toilet along the wall. A stack of fresh towels was on the counter by the sink. I ran my hands over them to discover they were soft, almost with a brand new feel to them. I closed the door behind me and took my clothes off, allowing them to heap on the floor.

Stepping into the shower stall, I turned the knob on to a rather strong flow of cold water. I was very glad that the water pressure was high enough for a shower the way I liked it. As I reached over to grab the bar of soap, I noticed something odd. The water falling from the showerhead and pelting my skin was getting warmer. Did this wonderful town have enough resources to allow for hot water showers for visitors on top of everything else? I hadn't cleaned myself in water heated by anything other than the sun since I left home. Even when I was growing up, hot showers were extremely rare. They were usually reserved for someone recovering from a serious illness or getting ready for very special occasions like family weddings. This was a treat I had never imagined in my wildest dreams.

I enjoyed the luxury of the hot shower only a little longer than it took to get myself clean. I dried off with the towels on the counter and ran my fingers through my lengthening hair to straighten it some and keep it from looking sloppy as it dried. I considered it likely this friendly town had a barber in addition to all the services I'd seen so far. Wrapping the towel around my waist, I stepped outside the bathroom and opened the closet Johan had said was full of clothes. There was a wide array of sizes and styles hanging across the small space. There was also a small set of drawers in the bottom of the closet. A quick check revealed pants and shorts in nearly as many sizes as the hanging shirts.

As I perused the wardrobe choices, I heard two distinct voices in a conversation coming from the living room where I had left Johan alone. I could just make out what they were saying. I eavesdropped as I selected something to wear.

"He's a visitor. You know the rules. He has to enter the arena and win before he can leave."

Johan was being firm with the other person. "He is a messenger. They are immune to the regulations regarding visitors. He has done us all a favor and you want to thank him by putting him in that place?"

"You just put forward the exemption for messengers yesterday. The council hasn't had a full vote on it yet. It's not officially in place yet."

Johan sighed impatiently. "Which is why I'm personally escorting him to the arena tonight. We will see what the other council members say about it with him right there."

"Fine. We will see what happens tonight. Just know, if he doesn't end up in the arena tonight, I will be doing what I can to get you removed from the council so things can be run properly in this town for once."

I heard the door open and slam shut as I hurried back into the bathroom to get dressed. As I put the clothes on, I considered what I had just heard. Apparently, I was supposed to be in some sort of arena. Could this be the entertainment Johan was intending to take me to? He seemed to feel I shouldn't be forced into the arena. Maybe he meant to take me along just to watch what happens there. While I had seen him wield quite a bit of authority over others, it seemed his power wasn't universal in Greenville. It was very unlikely I would be allowed to bring my bow or shotgun into the arena, as an observer or competitor, so I would have to pay a lot of attention to what was going on around me.

I carried my shoes and socks to the living room, briefly enjoying the soft carpet on my bare feet. I kept my thoughts quiet about the conversation I had accidentally overheard. I wondered if I could subtly find out more information from Johan before we went for a ride in his car. I rolled a single sock up and slipped my foot in. Innocently I asked, "What kind of entertainment are we going to see tonight?"

"Nothing too elaborate. Just some simple physical competitions."

"I didn't see any parks or theaters on my trip through town. Where do these competitions take place?"

Johan chuckled lightly. "I'm sure you saw the giant gray building when you first came into town. You'd have to be blind to not notice it, regardless of which route you used. Inside that is a domed arena we built with some scrap metal we found in an old rail yard near here."

"How often do these competitions take place?"

"Three nights a week. We work hard here and the competitions allow everyone to let off some steam. Competitors and observers alike are so exhausted at the end of the night that they don't have any energy to get in any trouble. Then they get up the next morning rested, refreshed, and ready for another day of hard work."

"Does anyone ever die in one of these competitions?"

"The opponents are given a chance to yield when first blood is drawn. Either side can also back out at any point. The object is to simply knock the other person unconscious. Even with all the opportunities to end the match with both competitors alive, deaths happen from time to time."

"Sounds rough. How do you choose who enters the arena?"

"We have our own methods. At the start of each night's events we ask for volunteers from the audience. In the rare times that crimes are committed, the accused can choose to prove their innocence in a trial or in the arena. Some criminals are sentenced to a number of matches in the arena if they choose a trial and are found guilty. There is also a set of matches determined ahead of time."

"What do the winners of the matches get?"

"It depends on why they are there. Volunteers get the next day off from work without losing any rations. Accused and sentenced criminals earn freedom with a victory. Others are given a special reward they are informed of before entering the arena."

While we talked, I had donned my second sock and both shoes. I finished lacing up the second shoe and stomped my foot to adjust how my foot sat in the cushioning. These were an extra pair of shoes I kept with me so the fit was nearly perfect. The act of stomping was a habit I developed when I had to adjust the way my foot sat in shoes that had been handed down to me from my brothers. The time it took me to adjust my shoes allowed me to mentally absorb Johan's answers to my questions. I could also match these thoughts with what I had overheard him and the other gentleman saying earlier. There was one other delay tactic I could employ without raising any suspicions.

"I haven't had anything to eat besides snacks for a couple days and I'm famished after that nap. Would it be possible to get a meal before we go?"

Johan turned towards the door and opened it for me to pass through first. "There isn't anything worth calling a meal in here and the entertainment is due to start soon. Food will be available at the arena. As my guest, you will be provided with as much or as little of it as you want. It's pretty good fare too. Chicken grilled over an open fire, steaks slow cooked for hours, smoked pork with a hint of spices. There's also creamed corn, green beans, mashed potatoes, and a fresh vegetable salad. Plenty of choices for any tastes and appetites."

Johan's listing of the menu options had me salivating. I decided I could at least end my hunger before finding out what he did or didn't have in store for me at the arena. I walked out the door and Johan closed it behind me. Johan climbed behind the steering wheel of the small car, I sat in the passenger seat. The seat seemed unusually comfortable and roomy for such a small vehicle. It was as though the car was bigger on the inside.

Johan drove us up and down a number of streets. It seemed like he was taking a distinctly indirect route despite mentioning earlier that the entertainment would start soon. Even when I could see the arena building, Johan's turns seemed to not go in the most efficient direction. If his intent was to get me lost, it was in vain. I was still able to track our location and my way back to the house from other landmarks I spotted on the way.

We eventually reached the large gray building. A few people were entering the building through a large set of double doors. Johan drove around to the opposite side of the square building. There were five cars similar to the one we were in parked outside a smaller single door. Apparently each member of the council had his or her own vehicle to reach the arena. Our arrival must have been timed for us to avoid seeing the other drivers outside.

Johan parked the silent car and we walked up to the door. The sounds of an excited crowd could be heard through the door itself. The noise was even louder once I opened the door. Johan smiled as we entered and started walking down a narrow hallway. It was no surprise that sounds carried so well in here; the inside of the structure looked to be the same gray blocks as the outside. When we reached the end of the hall, it opened into a large area with a domed cage arcing over the middle of it. The floor of the cage was covered with a layer of sawdust and dirt. A knee-high wall circled the cage about five feet away. Bleachers lined all the sides of the available area with one corner left open for some grills and fire pits. Between the fire pits and crowd, were a handful of tables covered in food. Every dish that Johan had described earlier was being sampled by the few people not cheering from the stands.

Johan and I walked along the front of the bleachers towards the food tables. He was greeting and waving to the people in the crowd. All were happily returning his greetings. One entire section stood up and cheered his name. I glanced away from the crowd to see what they were enjoying at the moment. Two shirtless men were squaring up to each other in the middle of the metal dome. Each man was in a stance I recognized as being from the martial arts. I had never studied any of the disciplines myself, but knew enough about it to know it when I saw it.

The men were simply sparring. They would approach each other and attempt to strike. Most of the time kicks and punches were blocked or dodged. If a solid hit connected, the crowd would loudly cheer, regardless of which fighter got to the other. There was no way to tell the fighters apart as they moved around the dome. It didn't seem to matter, as the entire crowd appeared to be cheering for both of them at the same time. I watched only as long as it took to reach the food-covered tables.

Johan and I each grabbed a plate and filled them with food from the platters being refreshed by the folks working the fire pits and grills. The sight and smells of the food made me realize how truly hungry I was. We carried our plates away from the tables to an area of the bleachers that was sectioned off from the others. Instead of the standard bench seats, this area had fifteen high-backed chairs. Eight of them were already filled. Johan led me to a pair of seats away from the others. Once we were seated, he lifted a tray from the armrest of the chair and set his food on it. He then peered at me until I had done the same. The town apparently thought very highly of their city council members to treat them so well on a regular basis.

Johan spoke between bites of his chicken,

"These seats are for council members and their guests. It's not totally unheard of for a sitting council member to invite a former member up here for old time's sake. They allow us a good view of the area and crowds as well as making sure the town's citizens can recognize us. We can also unofficially talk official town business without having to worry about being overheard. Would you excuse me for a minute?"

Johan got up and made his way to some of the seats occupied by other council members. He stood behind their chairs, leaning against the backs and speaking over the heads of the others. The noise of the crowd prevented me from hearing what was being said, but it was very clear that this was an important discussion and a heated argument. Angry gestures and sharp movements were passing around the small group. Johan remained calm through the entire discussion. He suddenly stood up. The others stopped speaking and focused on what Johan had to say. As soon as he had his say, Johan turned from the others before they could respond. This apparently meant the discussion was at an end. There was no way for me to tell if anything had been decided, but it was obvious nothing more would be said tonight.

Johan spoke to me as he sat back down. His voice was emotionally flat like he was suppressing some anger but was relieved at the same time. "As a visitor to our town, you would normally be entered into a fight yourself tonight. I recently proposed a new measure to the town laws that would exempt messengers from fighting in our cage. While this is being debated, I was able to get you a pass tonight because of the information you brought us. This means you can sit back and enjoy the show without having to worry about becoming a part of it."

I felt a combination of nervousness, curiosity, and relief as the sparring duo in the metal dome bowed to each other and shook hands. The crowd cheered as the fighters waved to them and walked from the dome. They easily climbed between the bars and stepped over the low wall to the hall Johan and I had entered through. A man in a bright red coat and top hat walked out of the hallway to make room for the fighters to enter. He entered the dome and walked directly to the center. Most of the crowd had fallen silent, but a few murmurs of conversation could still be heard. The man in the dome gestured for silence as he slowly circled to view the entire collection of observers. Gradually a pall of silence filled the large building.

The acoustics of the building allowed the man's voice to carry to everyone without requiring a microphone or speakers. "Ladies and gentlemen. Welcome to another night of action in the Gray Arena. We welcome the esteemed City

Council and their guests. We have some interesting matches ahead of us tonight. One bout in particular, I myself have been looking forward to seeing. First things first, though. Is there anyone who wishes to volunteer to step into the dome? Is anyone upset with the color of their neighbor's shutters?" There was a general round of laughter at this comment. The announcer slowly scanned the crowd, looking for any signs of someone willing to step into the arena. Apparently this was not the night for volunteers settling disputes between themselves in the arena.

"It looks like we don't have anyone volunteering to step into the ring tonight. Then we shall move on to the court mandated matches. We have five of them to look forward to tonight. One match is between a pair of women that are both here with a sentence of more than ten fights. One lucky lady will be leaving tonight a free woman; the other has a long line of opponents ahead of her. First though, is a match between two unfamiliar faces. Unless, that is, you've seen them committing the crimes they've been sentenced for. Fight fans, please welcome Ira 'Indecent Exposure' Johansen and Freddie 'The Flasher' Smith."

Two men were escorted by guards into the arena. I guessed the nicknames of the fighters hinted at their crimes. I was glad to see both of them entering the dome fully dressed. One came from the hallway I had used earlier, the other from a hallway on the opposite side of the arena. They were each escorted by two large muscular men with serious looks on their stony faces. The convicted men looked small and insignificant between their guards. The smaller men were hobbled by chains linked to cuffs around their wrists and ankles. When each trio reached the low wall, the guards lifted the convicted men over the wall and began removing their shackles. The men were now free to move as they entered the metal dome and walked to the center. The announcer spoke to them and then addressed the crowd again as he left the arena himself.

"You all know the rules. The victor is released with no record of this particular crime. The loser has one less fight to complete on his sentence. The standard rules apply for this bout. At the first sign of blood the bleeder will be given the chance to yield. If either man is down for more than ten seconds, he shall be considered defeated."

As the announcer left the dome, someone handed him a large bell. The announcer struck the bell and the sound echoed through the building as the two men began to fight. Men in the audience seemed to have picked their favorites for this match. Women seemed to be unimpressed as a group. I could only assume the ladies in the audience had seen too much of both of these men. The match itself was uneventful and I couldn't really tell which one was the victor. Three more criminal bouts followed, each one featuring increasingly bigger competitors and more severe crimes. The promised match between the women was the second to last fight and the most vicious. One had been accused of stealing from the community food storage. The other had been seen damaging public property at parks and the council office. The final bout was between two men accused of murder and attempted murder.

With the end of the criminal matches, the announcer returned to the center of the dome. As he began his next speech, a group of men entered the arena with large duffel bags on their shoulders. They each began to circle the dome and place items from inside their bags on the ground between the low wall and the metal dome. It took me a minute to realize the items were weapons. Axes, swords, knives of varying lengths, and poles in sections that were assembled before being placed on the ground. All the previous bouts between the citizens of Greenville had been in hand-to-hand combat. Now weapons were being brought in. I wondered how the combatants for these special bouts were chosen and why they required potentially lethal instruments.

The announcer was much more animated as he moved in the center of the dome. Instead of simply standing and turning to survey the crowd, this time he practically pranced and spun around the middle of the arcing dome. "Weren't those fun? I'm sure we will be seeing at least one of those victors here again before too much longer. Some people just can't seem to keep themselves out of trouble.

"Now we come to my personal favorite part of the night. I'm sure many of you enjoy it as well. Time for the Transients' Battles! One man gets to leave with his family; the other must stay and fight again. We give visitors all they could want while they are in Greenville; the least they can do is entertain us during their stay. Unfortunately, we only have a single bout tonight. We have seen both of these fighters before, though. They have grown more desperate and viscous with each fight they have lost. Will the guards please escort our combatants into the ring?"

The crowd absolutely erupted with noise. Both the men and the women in the audience screamed in joy and excitement. The announcer had fallen silent in anticipation of the racket and his inability to be heard over it. He was waving his arms and encouraging the crowd to get even louder as two men were led into the arena from the opposing hallways. The men looked similar in size and build. The only distinguishing features I could see were a blue shirt on one and a yellow shirt on the other. Instead of being lightly

49

shackled like the criminals were earlier, this time the combatants were bound and hooded. They were handcuffed behind their backs. The legs of the fighters were free, but it would take considerable effort for them to get anywhere quickly. The escorts had a tight grip on the fighters' elbows. The size difference between the combatants and escorts was minimal this time, despite the fact the escorts had been the same since the first bout.

The escorts and their charges stepped over the low wall with the ease of repeated practice. The confined fighters were escorted to the middle of the dome next to the joyous announcer. The crowd started to calm down. Johan nudged me with his elbow. I leaned over to better hear him speaking since the general noise was still so loud it made normal conversation difficult.

"Anyone that comes through town on their way somewhere else is given the best treatment. Each family gets a house similar to the one you slept in today. They are well fed and taken care of. The male leader or strongest member of each family is brought here to fight in exchange for the food and electricity they have consumed. The winner is returned to his family and they are led out of town and back on their journey the next morning. The loser is also returned to his family. However, they remain another day, using another allotment of food and electricity to be repaid with another fight."

I was becoming angry with Johan for bringing me to this violent event. I had been considering another trip to the food tables before the last fight started, but I had no appetite left now. How could he think I would enjoy watching this? Suddenly the conversation I overheard in the house made a lot more sense. "I heard what you told that other guy earlier. As a messenger, I am exempt from the required battles, thanks to you. However, that does not mean I have to like what I'm going to see."

"I don't want you to like it. It is evil and wrong. Visitors should be allowed to repay us with whatever they choose, not be forced to become subjects for our barbaric enjoyment. I want you to do more than see it. I want you to help me stop it. I can't do it myself. It would take longer than I have on the council to pass enough laws to change the very popular policies that keep this travesty going. That is assuming that I wouldn't get outvoted at every turn. My only hope is to get messengers exempted from fighting and get them to spread the word to surrounding towns. If we can get people to stop passing through here, the fights will be limited to volunteers and criminals. Over time, even those sources will dry up and the fights will stop completely."

I could understand what Johan was trying to do. It would take a considerable amount of time for the word to spread to all surrounding towns and villages and from there to any travelers passing through the area. However, letting messengers through would speed the process up significantly. With a purely mechanical interest, I turned back to the dome as the crowd finally quieted down enough for the announcer to have his say.

"Ladies and gentlemen. We are proud to bring you the final fight of the night. These two men have each been here at least five times. They have lost to many opponents. Their only reason for fighting is for the freedom of their loved ones who are resting comfortably. Shall we all see how much they love their families? How much they really want to leave our fine town?"

The announcer raised his hands in the air and the crowd roared again as the escorts tore the hoods from the men due to fight. A rope was tied around each man's wrists and the handcuffs were removed. The men stood still and glared at the audience and announcer as the escorts backed out of the dome, trailing the other end of the rope around the men's wrists along with them. Once the escorts were out of the low concrete wall ringing the dome, they gave the ropes a quick jerk. This pulled the ropes free and released the men from their bindings. Both men were now free to move about the inside of the metal dome and do what they could to get their families free from this demented town.

The men rubbed their wrists and sized each other up for a moment before either made a definitive move. The man in the yellow shirt dropped his arms to his sides and stared at the one in blue. Yellow Shirt then suddenly ran directly at him with one arm out in an attempt to clothesline Blue Shirt. Blue ducked under the extended arm and rolled to one side. Yellow didn't stop after his missed attack, which was apparently really a feint. He kept running to the side of the dome where he reached through the bars to grab one of the weapons that had been laid out earlier. His first choice was a long metal staff with sharp points at each end. Unfortunately, the staff was longer than the gap in the bars was wide. Yellow was jerked off his feet as the staff clanged loudly against the bars of the dome. The crowd reacted with a mixture of cheers, taunts and laughter.

Blue took a second after his roll on the ground to locate his opponent. He saw Yellow drop to the ground with the staff still in his hand. Blue ran to the opposite side of the dome and quickly looked over his weapon options there. He reached down and grabbed a small axe in each hand. The axes weren't large enough to make any trees shake in fear, but they could still easily do significant damage to any human body parts in their way. He walked confidently back across the dome spinning the axes in his hands and swinging them in quick, powerful arcs.

The entire audience, me included, was mesmerized by the fighters' actions. It seemed like the only breaths being taken in the entire building were those of the men in the dome. The people working the fire pits and grills had pulled everything off the heat and were standing still as they too focused on the fight before them. Both of the fighters strongly wanted to leave and had been denied the chance to do so over and over because of their own weaknesses. All of that frustration was going to be released tonight.

Yellow turned his staff and got it inside the dome before Blue could reach him. He had to quickly roll out of the way as Blue swung both axes down hard, the sharp blades biting into whatever was under the sawdust on the floor. Yellow stood up and got into a defensive stance with the staff in front of him before Blue could yank his axes free of the floor. I didn't get the impression that either fighter was a professional, but their moves were practiced from their recent experiences in this domed cage.

Blue stormed at Yellow, raising his axes overhead again to swing them down in another powerful arc. This time Yellow lifted his staff up to block his opponent's attack. The handles of both axes struck the staff, the heads stopping mere inches from Yellow's face. The sound of the metal on metal rang out around the inside of the arena, the shape of the room creating a chiming echo. Neither fighter showed any sign of the vibrations, although I was sure both felt them running through their hands and up their arms.

Yellow pushed the axes up and away from him then swept one end of the staff at Blue's foot. The sweep missed, but Blue was forced to take a step back in order to keep his balance. The fighters now stood a small distance from each other. Blue had one arm raised across his chest, axe ready to be swung down from his other shoulder. The other axe was in a tight grip, his knuckles white. Yellow was in a stable stance with his feet apart some and the staff being held diagonally across his body. As the men gauged each other from a short distance, I couldn't help but wonder why neither used their weapons to escape the arena and run off with their families.

Johan must have anticipated my question as I leaned over to ask him. Without taking his eyes off the fight, he answered me before I could say anything. "The doors are locked so nobody comes in or out of the building until the bouts are over. Even if a visiting fighter does get out, the routes back to the homes we use for transients are indirect intentionally. The most direct routes have roadblocks of debris piled in the streets. You would have to know the exact turns to take in order to get from here to there. Assuming someone gets outside and manages to navigate their way to the house with their families, there is still one more safeguard. The families are guarded and can be moved at a moment's notice. One blast of a horn here at the arena and the house the family is in is vacated and they are confined somewhere else."

The men had circled each other while Johan spoke to me. I would be able to leave Greenville in the morning and be on my way. These men had been here for days with their families in a strange home, not knowing when and if they were going to be able to leave. Johan had mentioned that death wasn't the object of the fights, but I'm sure some families were concerned their loved ones might not even come home. The crowd was getting bored with the stalled action and had started booing and yelling suggestions to the fighters. With both combatants armed, I expected the bout to end quickly once one man decided to end the defensive standoff and go on the attack. The audience would get the blood and action it desired.

Yellow swung the low end of his staff up at Blue, who easily deflected it with the head of his lowered axe. Yellow attacked with the ends of his staff, alternating between them, back and forth, right and left, up and down. Blue deflected most of the attacks with swings of his axes. What he didn't block, he dodged with movements of his upper body. The patterns of Yellow's attempts to attack became quickly predictable, however, they were coming so fast and close together, it was extremely difficult for Blue to find a gap in which to counterattack. Yellow's attempts to attack suddenly ceased and he took a step back. It appeared Yellow had just been testing Blue's defenses with attacks he knew wouldn't land.

Blue then took his turn to attack. He started with a series of axe slashes that crossed his body. The blade of an axe would swing at Yellow from right shoulder to left hip and left shoulder to right hip. Yellow deflected each swipe a little with a tap of his staff. The attacks were sent wide of their target with a light ringing off the metal of the staff. Without missing a beat, Blue suddenly started swinging the axe in his right hand horizontally. He swung the axe back and forth repeatedly, stepping forward each time he reversed the blade's direction. The axe in Blue's left hand was raised to his left shoulder and ready to counterattack if Yellow made a move between swipes. If Yellow hadn't been stepping back with his staff at the ready, the strength and speed of Blue's attacks would have spread Yellow's intestines across the floor of the dome. As it was, no blood was being spilled at the moment.

Blue stopped for a minute to catch his breath. The crowd had been getting excited while each fighter tested the defenses of the other. They were quickly calming down again and getting upset at the lack of bloodshed so far.

Yellow decided to try another tactic. He changed his grip on his staff and hefted it like a spear. He hurled the staff at Blue, aiming for the center of his chest. The tip of the staff tore through Blue's shirt as he tried to dodge the projectile. He avoided being scratched himself by mere centimeters. He turned back towards Yellow just in time to receive a follow-up attack. Yellow had started running at Blue the moment he released the staff. Once he was within range, he balled up his fist, pulled his arm back, and let fly with a powerful punch that connected with all the force he could muster combined with the speed of his running charge. Blue fell to the ground on his back. He was stunned for a second as his axes fell from his hands.

The roar from the crowd was louder than anything I had heard so far. The announcer had to struggle to make himself heard. "Ladies and gentlemen. We have first blood. Does the competitor yield?"

It was only as the announcer was saying it that I noticed a steady trickle of blood coming out of Blue's nose as he lay on the ground groaning. Yellow was standing back against the far side of the dome, waiting to see if Blue would get up and continue the fight. Some members of the crowd were holding their breath as they waited for Blue to rise, others chanted for the fight to resume.

Blue looked to be recovering from the strike gradually. The noises from the audience prevented me from hearing it, but I got the distinct impression Blue moaned as he sat up. Yellow moved away from the edge of the arena until he was mere inches from standing directly over Blue. One glance to each side told Blue that he could only reach one of the axes on the ground beside him before Yellow could reach the other. There was no advantage to arming himself at the moment.

Blue carefully backed away from Yellow as he stood up. Yellow let his opponent get off the ground and get himself ready. Blue gave his head a shake to clear it. He then took an aggressive stance with both hands clenched into tight fists and raised up ready to strike Yellow.

The announcer did his best to signal everyone to be quiet. "Ladies and gentleman, first blood has been drawn. It appears the wounded fighter has opted not to yield. Let me hear what you think of his decision!"

The audience seemed to be trying to knock the walls down with the strength of their voices. Johan and I were the only ones not adding our shouts to the ruckus. The fighters stepped closer to each other and began throwing punches. Blows were landed on each man's body and attacks to the head were either dodged or blocked. The lack of major fighting experience was more obvious when the men fought hand-to-hand than it was when they are armed. There were no martial arts being utilized here, just two men brutally attacking each other with animalistic fury.

Sweat was starting to soak the fighters' shirts as they once again stepped back from each other. Yellow's hands were hanging limply at his sides. Blue was struggling to keep his hands up to block any more attempts from Yellow to take advantage of any signs of weakness. Both men were very clearly exhausted. The only thing I could see keeping them on their feet was their love for their respective families and the desire to take them safely away from the town of Greenville. There was no anger in the men's eyes, just determination and focus on the unfortunate task at hand.

The crowd cheered the men on as they went at each other with more vigor than their respective levels of exhaustion should have permitted. I watched the fighters and the crowd as more punches and poorly aimed kicks were thrown back and forth. The fight seemed to stretch on longer and longer. The small remnants of food next to me sat unforgotten and unappetizing. My mouth was too dry to eat anyway. The rest of the crowd seemed to enjoy it the longer the fight lasted. Roars and cheers erupted as particularly hard blows were landed. Blood started oozing from cuts on both fighters' faces and hands. Tears were developing in their shirts and marks had appeared on their faces and arms that would no doubt become dark bruises later.

As the fight dragged on, I watched less of the combatants and more of the crowd. They cheered more for the violence than for either particular fighter. I did notice someone would occasionally shake their head or look slightly disappointed when one fighter or another received a particularly hard blow or staggered for a few steps. I turned to Johan and this time he let me ask my question, "Is there any gambling on these fights?"

Johan turned to me with a look that practically shouted his disappointment in the other residents of this town. "Because of the chances for throwing a match, none of the early fights can be bet on. Wagers can only be placed on the fighters struggling to leave town. Bets are made with food items or hours to be worked. We use cash so rarely, some people bet with it only as a joke."

The fighters continued to struggle against each other to the assembled crowd's delight and entertainment. Yellow managed to knock Blue down for a fourth time. This time, Blue didn't struggle to get up. Blue leapt at Yellow as soon as the standing man's guard was down. His momentum and the element of surprise at the sudden attack knocked Yellow hard against the bars of the domed cage. Blue simply stood and watched as Yellow fell face first to the ground. Yellow lay still on the floor of the cage, his body moving faintly as he continued to breathe. At least it appeared he was still alive.

Blue stood there, breathing heavily and watching his opponent carefully. Yellow didn't attempt to roll himself over or even turn his head and get his face out of the dirt. Two of the guards from earlier stepped to the edge of the cage closest to Blue. He stepped back and relaxed his stance as a woman quickly entered the cage and went directly to Yellow's prone form. I didn't realize what she was doing until Johan explained it to me.

"That's our town's top physician. We call her Doctor Liz. She's giving him a quick check to determine whether or not he can keep fighting. The guards that escorted that man in earlier will carry him to her office where she will care for his more serious injuries. She will make sure he is healthy enough to fight before he enters the ring again. With the conditions I've seen some of the men in when she ended the combat, I think she is growing to dislike these fights as much as

I do. Either that, or she is just being lazy and removing the men from the fight before they can suffer any injury serious enough for her to have to work hard to heal. Because of the popularity of the fights and the excitement you have seen here, I am afraid to ask her which exactly it is."

Doctor Liz gave thumbs up to the announcer who was looking at her anxiously. Without waiting for him to acknowledge, she waved to two more men I hadn't noticed. They ran to the cage with a stretcher carried between them. With practiced movements, the two men rolled Yellow onto the stretcher, carried him to the edge of the cage, and exited without aggravating any of the unconscious man's wounds. Doctor Liz followed them closely and did her best to monitor Yellow's vital signs while on the move.

All of this went unnoticed by the crowd as the announcer declared Blue the winner. The cheers nearly drowned him out as he went over the very practiced lines stating what Blue had won and that he and his family would be leaving town in the morning. I only hoped Doctor Liz would be able to give him a brief examination and make sure he didn't end up worse off than Yellow, medically speaking.

Johan and I sat patiently as the crowds made their way out of the door in a mob-like fashion. While we waited for the crowd to thin out and during the drive back to the house I was assigned for the night, I composed the message I would be sending out from the next town. I would mark this message for other messengers to copy and distribute as far and wide as possible. Recommendations would be made that no more travelers should come through Greenville. It was only on extremely rare occasions like this that I wished for one form or another of a larger national government like my parents told me existed before the Exodus.

METROPOLIS

The next few days passed in an uneventful pattern. Ride in peace, stop and have lunch from the supplies with me, ride further, stop to hunt for dinner, sleep by a low campfire, wake up and have some leftover meat for breakfast, and begin riding again. It was a relaxing section of roads and passages. I felt more content than I had in a very long time. While I certainly enjoyed the beauty of the nature around me and the flexibility of being alone, I would have liked to have someone to share it with.

The only thing that changed was the scenery as I approached the first site of a former major metropolis along my route, St. Louis, Missouri. The city's trademark arch was still standing, looking a little worn and dirty. I stopped to marvel at its magnificence before making my way across one of the last standing bridges in the area spanning the Mississippi River.

The city itself was mostly empty. The few remaining residents tended to live at the edges of the city, where the ground was more workable than amongst the steel, glass, and concrete of the city center. Many of the large buildings I passed were empty and some showed signs of vandals and squatters. I'm sure more than a handful of buildings were used as locations for thieves to stash their ill-gotten gains, most of which was sure to be useless anyway. Gold chains and expensive electronics meant little to someone wishing to trade for food or supplies to repair their home. Soft silks didn't make for decent work clothes. Chances are, if it was left behind when the Arks departed, it wasn't worth much to begin with.

I continued through the streets of St. Louis towards the setting sun. With some daylight left, I happened to spot a building with a clear mark painted on its door. It was the symbol used to mark a safe house for messengers on their travels. There wouldn't be any food or supplies inside, but it would be a decent shelter for the night and common convention meant I would be safer from thieves than in the empty vaults and penthouses of the rest of the city. I walked my bike inside the building and found an empty room near the entrance. I lifted the saddlebags from my bike and placed them near a soft looking sofa. I also unstrapped a toolkit from under the seat. In a series of well-practiced movements, I flipped my bicycle over and set it on the floor upside down. Sitting down, I opened the toolkit and began a careful inspection of my bike. A couple of bolts were a tad loose, but showed no signs of wear that would mean they required immediate replacement. The tires still had plenty of tread on them and hadn't picked up any sharp objects that would puncture an inner tube over time. I lay down on the couch once my maintenance work was done. Sleep quickly came over me before the sun completely vanished past the horizon.

That night was a restless one. I slept lightly despite the safety promised by the mark outside the door. An empty building has dangers besides those presented by other humans. My sleep was also interrupted by sounds that were familiar yet still seemed strange. Vehicles periodically rumbled past the building. Shouting voices echoed between the buildings around the one I slept in. It was impossible for me to make out what was being said, but the tones clearly weren't friendly. The occasional crack of gunfire reinforced this impression. Even though the violence wasn't aimed at me, I still feared for the person that was their potential or current victim.

I finally awoke shortly before the sun made its daily appearance. I turned my bike back onto its tires and replaced my saddlebags and toolkit. I walked to the door and stood in the entrance, listening carefully to the awakening world. Remounting the seat, I started pedaling west again, moving easily through the otherwise empty city streets. There were no signs of the violence that interrupted my rest the previous night.

There were still a number of ways across the former state of Missouri with and without crossing the Missouri river. Unfortunately, a number of these routes were inaccessible or used roads that had been washed away by repeated floods or destroyed by tornadoes. The notes on my maps indicated that the best possible route was to cross the Missouri River here in St. Louis and again in Kansas City. The highway between the two cities was a straight path across the state. Many messengers had told me that the bridges were being maintained by locals in order to facilitate their own transportation of goods around this rich farming area.

I angled myself North as I moved further into the city. The streets made traveling easier, even though it meant taking a less than direct route to the Northwest corner of the city. Three bridges crossed the river there. Should one be in too poor a condition to cross, I still had two options to choose from. It was early afternoon when I came to the first bridge. It was almost completely destroyed. Support structures rose from the flowing waters and ended abruptly. The road under me ended some distance before it reached the far bank of the river. I didn't stop long enough or get close enough to determine if it was knocked down intentionally or just fell from disrepair.

The next bridge was in a similar condition. This time the roadway ended at a jagged edge hanging over the water. Concrete pilings stood from the waters below, their tops empty and visibly crumbling.

I reached the area of the third bridge shortly before evening. I decided to rest one more night here rather than approach the bridge in the dark. If this one was as damaged as the other two, then it would be easier to find an alternate route in the daylight. I spotted a collection of buildings with a handful of them still intact. The signs on the road and buildings seemed to indicate it was a small airport. More than a couple of the intact structures had tall grass in front of their doors, indicating a lack of traffic in or out. It seemed I should be able to safely rest in one of the hangars or mechanical storage sheds.

I decided to go without a fire for the night. The overnight temperatures were still high enough for me to be comfortable with just a blanket for warmth. There were also some barrels of fuel in the building I had decided to camp in. An open flame was simply too much risk, even though the airport had been long abandoned. After a cold dinner, I settled down for some restful slumber. The sound of the river flowing nearby alternated with the wind in the leaves to sing me to sleep.

The singing of birds welcoming the day

quickly woke me as the sun started to peek its way above the horizon. After another cold breakfast, I made my way across the tarmac to the road leading to the bridge across the river. I spotted what appeared to be damaged road signs on each side of the route in the low early morning light. The brightening sky above revealed what the tall poles really were. They were warnings to wary travelers. Human heads on wooden pikes had apparently been broadcasting a clear message for decades. The path ahead was a dangerous one to visitors and strangers. Despite this, I kept moving forward. I hoped my status as a messenger would keep me safe in this clearly violent area. I didn't need much protection, just enough to get across the bridge and on with my journey.

My luck was just slightly better at the third bridge. The majority of the bridge was still intact. The road stretched across the running water from the opposite bank. Unlike the other two bridges, the end of the road was clean and smooth. No jagged or crumbling asphalt there. However, the road on this bank ended abruptly. It looked like someone had lifted a section of the bridge clean out of the water.

I was about to turn around and find a spot to update my local maps when I heard a familiar sound echoing in the morning air. It was a sound I had heard only occasionally growing up on the farm. I recognized it from the night before last while I slept inside the safe house. It was the steady thrum of a gasoline engine. It was getting louder as the engine got closer. Not only was the sound getting louder, it was also becoming obvious that there was more than one vehicle approaching the bridge and its missing segment. The combination of vehicles sounded very similar to the ones I had heard roaming the empty streets during my restless sleep in the building in the middle of the city. However, this time there were no shouts or sounds of gunfire.

The piked heads on the road and the fact the vehicles were deliberately headed to this dead end told me that these people knew more about the area than I did. Some inner instinct told me that me being a messenger was something that would only be discovered after it was too late to save me from a fate similar to those back up the road. A sense of fear mixed with a degree of curiosity about the people that could perpetrate such violence and not wipe themselves out within a couple of years, made me want to see these people more closely from a discreet distance. I picked up my bike and carried it as I ran to the edge of the road. There were numerous trees on each side of the road, plenty of places for me to hide until the oncoming vehicles left. I managed to get myself and my bike out of sight before the roaring became visible vehicles. I could still see the disconnected ends of the bridge and areas around the opposite side from my hiding place. As long as nobody in the vehicles looked directly towards me, they wouldn't know I was there.

As the vehicles came into sight, I could tell they had been modified. The three cars and one pickup truck looked nothing like the abandoned cars and trucks I had seen around my hometown and parked on the sides of some of the larger highways I had ridden across. These had sheets of metal neatly attached over the windows. There was a person armed with a machine gun sticking out of the roof of each car. There were two guys standing carefully balanced in the back of the pickup. Each of them was armed with a machine gun in their hands and what appeared to be shotguns holstered to their backs. Everybody I could see was carefully looking around. Their hands weren't gripping the triggers of their weapons, but they were held close enough to quickly fire off a few rounds at a second's notice. It was clear this was no simple group out for a leisurely drive; they had violence in mind. What I couldn't figure out was whom they intended to be so violent to. They were the only people I had seen in a week; there was nobody around for them to victimize.

I kept myself absolutely still as the vehicles approached the end of the road. A large individual got out of the lead car. He was both tall and stoutly built. He didn't so much step out of the door as he extracted himself from the side of it. He walked to the very edge of the road. The river was flowing strongly far below his feet. After a few seconds of staring across the water he turned to the vehicles, looked stonily at them, and turned back to the opposite side of the river. He bellowed in a voice that seemed to come from deep within the earth itself. I could hear his words echoing off the far bank as clearly as though I was right in front of him. He was calling for someone named Jack to get his hands out of his pants and raise the Goddamn bridge. The threats being made to Jack's person if he didn't get moving were enough to make my skin crawl. If I hadn't been doing my best to keep still and avoid notice, I would have cringed with each word on Jack's behalf.

The leader stopped his bellowing and caught his breath; he was winded from projecting his voice and rage across the river. His face reddened from his breathing, his obvious anger, or a mixture of both. Even the river seemed quieter for a few seconds as the leader seemed to consider the lack of reaction from Jack or anyone else on the other side of the river. Suddenly his hand thrust up into the air. Almost as one unit, the entire group of vehicles started blaring their horns. The racket seemed to draw more attention than the leader's voice did. Heads started popping out of windows in the buildings across the river. More than one person's head quickly ducked back inside. The leader dropped his arm, silencing the horns, as soon as people started emerging from the doors of the buildings.

A single figure ran out onto the bridge from the other side of the river and opened the door to a small hut tucked against the steel overhead support structure of the middle of the bridge. Another person was bodily tossed from the hut and lay, barely moving, on the asphalt. I guessed this was the unfortunate Jack, but truly hoped it wasn't, for the sake of his continued existence. The active figure entered the hut and I heard the mechanical sound of gears shifting. Gradually a sturdy wooden platform rose on cables from the mud and silt of the riverbed. The platform's size and shape fit perfectly into the missing segment of the bridge. I could just see that it was suspended from nearly invisible cables hanging from the other end of the bridge. It was easy to assume that there were similar cables under the end that Mr. Violence was now standing on. Whatever mechanism I was hearing was most likely retracting these cables, lifting the platform into place. It was a rather ingenious modernization of the medieval drawbridge method for protecting one's town. As the platform rose to its place, two more figures started across the bridge from the far side. They reached the collapsed individual on the ground and lifted him up. There were no signs of life from the body they now held dangling between them.

The leader started storming his way across the bridge as soon as the platform settled into place and the gears ceased their noise. The cars formed a single line behind him and carefully began crossing the bridge. They spaced themselves so that no more than one car was on the platform at a time. Their spacing was so precise and smooth, it was clear they had done this many times before. Gears began grinding again and the platform started lowering as soon as the trailing pickup truck had all four tires off of the drawbridge and onto the permanent bridge itself.

The leader reached the unconscious figure suspended between the two other men and stopped. The cars moved past the small group and sped to the far bank. The leader's hand shot out and grabbed the man I assumed was Jack by the throat. Holding Jack's limp form at arm's length, the leader's other arm swung around and hit Jack across the face with an open palm. I could hear the smack across the river from my hiding place. It was this sudden impact that seemed to bring Jack back to the world of the living, if only briefly. Jack groggily looked the leader up and down. From my hiding spot I couldn't tell if he was sleepy, drunk, or high on some drug. Whatever the reason, I didn't think he would want to be too awake or sober for what was bound to happen next.

The large group leader pulled his empty hand back and swung his fist forward hard and fast enough at Jack's body to break a couple of ribs. I'm sure Jack would have collapsed back to the ground if he weren't still supported by the other two men. Two more hard punches assaulted Jack's torso before the leader released his neck. A gesture to the hut brought out the person inside. He was carrying a rope or cable of some sort. A sense of dread and pity for Jack started to rise in me. One end of the rope was already suspended from one of the cross beams of the steel support structure of the bridge. The leader used his fist to club Jack across the face hard enough to permanently affect his vision and breathing. My dread grew as the leader reached for the rope being brought to him and started looping it around Jack's neck. He wrapped Jack's neck in a number of loose loops instead of a hangman's noose. It was clear that it was not intended to be a quick and easy death.

The person that had brought out the rope returned to the hut. Once the leader was satisfied with the coils around Jack's neck, he gestured towards the hut again. Another set of gears started to whir and grind. This time the platform remained down as the rope around Jack's neck started becoming taut. It wasn't long before the two guys were no longer holding Jack up between them. His entire weight was now being supported by the coiled loops tightening around his neck. The gears stopped once Jack was dangling high enough for his feet to be at the eye level of the group of observers watching from the ground. I was horrified yet unable to look away. The few faces I could see from across the river had mixed emotions. Some seemed almost as appalled as I was; others appeared to be enjoying the activity like it was some sort of show for their entertainment.

Despite his earlier lack of motion, Jack now moved quite a bit as his body struggled to live. I finally forced myself to turn away and stop watching this extended cruelty. I knew how Jack was going to come to his end. What I didn't want to know was how they were going to dispose of the body.

After a period of time that seemed to stretch into an eternity, the faint sounds I could hear of Jack's struggling faded away. I looked back at the group on the bridge. Jack was once again completely still, his body swinging slightly with the momentum caused by his struggles. The leader watched his former bridge operator sway back and forth a few times. His next move both surprised me and explained some of the heads on pikes that lined the road. He leaped up and wrapped his arms around Jack's legs, adding his significant weight to the strain on the rope around Jack's neck. I'm glad my distance prevented me from hearing the sound as Jack's head and neck finally and violently separated. The leader landed on his feet and maintained his balance with practiced motions.

He then dragged Jack's body past the steel supports of the bridge to the abrupt end of the pavement. I had failed to notice the dark brown smears on the road surface until I saw the blood flowing from Jack's body adding to them. The leader began to spin around in well-practiced motions. The momentum lifted Jack's limp body into the air until it was sticking straight out from the leader's twirling form. With a grunt, he flung the headless corpse into the river then turned back to walk across the bridge towards the buildings just before the body splashed into the flowing water. If this was how such a minor offense like passing out on the job was handled by this leader, I would hate to see how theft or murder was punished. Assuming such acts weren't encouraged in a community led by such a figure, that is.

I remained still until I saw the group on the bridge enter buildings or disappear around street corners. Those watching from inside the buildings had all retreated before Jack's body hit the water. While I was sure I could escape before the lowered section of the bridge could be raised again, I wasn't sure I could outrun their vehicles long enough to get to another place to hide. Even the figure in the hut left after a minute and entered one of the buildings on the other side of the river. Apparently nobody else would need access to the bridge via the platform any time soon. I decided to wait until dark to leave my hiding position just in case. In the meantime, I studied my maps for an alternate route to Kansas City and beyond. I also made certain to note the destroyed bridges and circled the area opposite me as a large "No Go" zone.

After the sun set, I carried my bike and moved through the trees back towards the road that led to the bridge. I mounted the road as far from the bridge as possible and rode my bike back to the airport I had bunked in the night before. Apparently Jack's head would be taken care of later as it was still hanging from the rope when I left. I was disgusted by the depths humanity could still reach. The only saving grace was that this group was isolated. As much as I didn't want to believe it, there seemed to be some validity to what some people said about the best parts of our species having left on the Arks.

VACANT

I found myself on the top of a tall hill, looking over a small town tucked into the valley below. It seemed an ideal small community. The road I was on led down to a central main street between two rows of shops. None of the buildings were more than two stories tall. The only thing that sat any higher was the steeple of the church. I could see it reaching into the heavens near the other side of the valley, a couple of blocks off of the central road. Small residences spread out even further than I could see. Numerous small homes surrounded by well-kept yards reached beyond the edges of the valley. Small lanes connected everything like the strands of a spider's web. Tracts of farmland edged the bases of the hills that surrounded the valley. I had seen some more of the farms on the other side of the hill that gave me this wonderful view. The entire town looked like it was pulled directly out of one of the books of fine paintings from the past that my parents had.

Despite the beauty and welcoming nature of the scene before me, something seemed a little odd and unnerving. It took me a few minutes to realize exactly what was making me feel uneasy as I rode into the town. There were absolutely no people. Despite the nice day and comfortable temperature, nobody was walking the sidewalks or browsing the shops. Not a single person could be seen tending their yard. Windows on a couple of the homes I passed were open, but I couldn't see anyone preparing a meal or tidying the house.

The town didn't appear to be abandoned. I had passed through a handful of vacant towns so far. They all showed the same signs of decay. None of those signs were present here. The buildings were all in good repair. Windows were all intact and clean. All of the doors I could see were closed, none of them hanging loose on their hinges or sitting open. Items in the windows of the shops looked new. They hadn't been ravaged by looters or time. No leaves had piled up in the streets from years of neglect. The sidewalks were free of dust and no weeds had grown up in the cracks. The fields I had passed approaching town were well maintained. The soil looked healthy and weeds hadn't been allowed to grow rampantly through the crops.

Someone was clearly living here and maintaining everything. They had either vanished or gone into hiding. There were no obvious signs of someone moving a curtain aside to watch me. No human-shaped shadows lurked around the corner of any of the buildings. No eyes peeked from inside a darkened home through the crack of an opened door. No parents hurried their scampering children off the street in front of me. No sounds of whispered conversation drifted on the breeze moving through the valley. The only signs of human life were its glaring absence.

I could hear the sounds of animals moving through some brush in the distance. Small groups of birds took wing from the tops of buildings as I entered the center of town. It seemed like I was moving through a ghost town that even the ghosts had forgotten.

I reached the center of town where most communities had boards with messages that they needed carried on to other towns. There was a board in this town as well. However, this board was completely devoid of any messages. There were no messages in the slots waiting to be taken. No packages sat under the board for delivery to distant friends or family. Even the box where incoming messages were placed was empty.

I leaned my bike against the board and sat down at the base of a nearby statue that marked the center of town. It was some long-dead town hero staring off towards the horizon. I noticed but didn't read the brightly polished brass plaque at the hero's feet. I rummaged and sorted through my maps until I was able to locate this town on one of them. I found it only on one small map of the immediate region. I circled the town and the farmlands I had seen on the way. I then crossed out the town's name on my map and wrote Ghost Town. After a minute of thought, I added a couple of question marks after the name.

As I picked up my bike, an idea struck me. I wrote a note with my thoughts on this town and put it in a slot for any other messengers going east. I also added a comment that this town should probably be avoided unless a message needed to be delivered to this specific place. I would place a similar message on the board of the next occupied town I entered to the west. I thought that if the people of this town wanted to be left alone this much, diverting messengers away from here would be doing them a favor. If there truly was nobody left in this town, then I was doing other messengers a favor by making them aware there was nothing here for them. Either way, I figured I was making things easier for everyone involved.

I got back on my bike and started to ride out of town on the main road that had carried me in. The weird sense of strangeness began to recede and the hairs on the back of my neck started to lay back down as I got closer to leaving this eerily quiet valley.

MISSING DAYS

Darkness and light. Alternating periods of darkness and light. The last thing I remembered was riding down a long hill on my way towards a village on the western end of the state of Colorado. I sped hard into a section of tree lying across the road and was tossed over my handlebars and onto the pavement. Then just cycles of darkness and light with occasional voices mixed in. Either I couldn't hear the voices or just didn't understand them in my condition.

I had no clue how I got from there to the soft bed I later found myself in. Whoever found my injured form certainly wanted me to be comfortable while I healed. The sun was streaming in through a window across from where I lay. I had no way of knowing if it was an early morning sun or the shine from the late afternoon. The fact I wasn't hungry meant one of two things: either not much time had passed since my accident or my caretakers had found a way to feed me during my periods of unconsciousness.

I slowly sat up and looked around. My clothes were neatly folded and piled on a chair in the corner of the nice-sized bedroom. I was still wearing my underwear, so I was able to keep some degree of modesty. Someone had tended to wounds I didn't realize I had until I saw the bandages and creams on them. The bandages covered larger scratches and sections of road rash. The creams were smeared on smaller cuts here and there on my arms. There was also a damp cloth on my forehead, probably put there to help fight a fever from infection. The longer I sat here, the more my mind seemed to clear.

I turned and set my legs on the floor. There was a rug next to the bed that kept my feet from feeling the cold of the bare hardwood floor. I tried to stand up and immediately felt light-headed. I sat back down hard on the soft mattress, fighting to stay awake amidst the darkness pressing at the edges of my vision. I had never felt such a strong wave of weakness before. While I waited for full consciousness to return to me, I slowly ran my hand over my head. There was a significant bump on the back of my head and a slightly smaller one near my right temple. This explained the damp towel on my head better than the chance of infection from my smaller and less life-threatening wounds.

The door to the bedroom opened and a young woman entered just as I was feeling like myself again. Her voice was gentle and smooth. "I see you are awake. It probably isn't a good idea to try to get up too fast. It looked like you had a rather hard knock on your head," she said as she set a water pitcher and a bowl of something steamy and delicious smelling down on the nightstand next to the bed. She smoothed her slightly stained white apron and simple dress as she continued, "We tended to your wounds and kept you warm in the hopes you would heal."

"How long have I been here?"

"Not very long. My aunt found you early in the afternoon the day before yesterday. My sisters and I brought you here that evening and started bandaging your cuts and scrapes. This is the most awake and talkative you've been since then." She ran her hands through her long, golden hair, which framed a round, slightly tanned face. I appreciated her classic yet wholesome beauty.

"What about my bike? Did you leave it by the log I hit?"

"No. We figured you were doing something important by the way you were traveling. My aunt brought your bike back while the rest of us carried you. It will need some repairs before you can travel any further though."

"How bad is the damage?"

"Some cosmetic scrapes, about like you, really. However, the front wheel is severely dented and the handlebars are bent. Any other alignment damage would be up to you to find.

You probably won't be able to find any replacement parts here, but there is a small town about a day's walk north that should have anything you need."

"Thank you for all that you and your family have done."

"You are most certainly welcome. Now, it's time for you to have something to eat. This is a thick broth that we've been feeding you since you got here. Would you like me to feed you again, or do you think you are up to doing it yourself?"

I wasn't sure, but her tone of voice seemed to hint that there was more than food being offered. "Thank you, but I think I would like to try to feed myself, see how much of my strength I have back."

"Okay. It shouldn't be too hot to eat right away. I didn't realize you would be awake so I let it cool before bringing it up.

Reaching underneath the bed, she pulled out a tray and set it on my lap as I positioned myself more completely on the bed. Once I was settled, she placed the bowl on the tray and pulled a spoon from a pocket of her apron. The soup was rather thick and creamy. It tasted cheesy with a hint of garlic. There was also a mixture of other flavors I couldn't quite name. There didn't seem to be any chunks of meat or pieces of vegetable in the soup. The texture reminded me of the potato chowder my mother was fond of making.

The young woman pulled a glass off the nightstand. She filled it with water from the pitcher she had brought in with her as she explained, "It is a blend of helpful herbs in a cheese soup that comes from an old family recipe. We make it thick enough to fill the stomach during a long convalescence. It's good enough that we eat it as part of our regular meals now and then. Goes well with the bread we make and some of the pork we trade with nearby farms for."

"It's quite good. Thank you again for taking care of me and providing me with this fine meal. Once I am up and around, is there anything I can do for you?"

"From all the letters in your vest, I guessed you are a messenger. We really don't have much need for you since our family is all on nearby farms. While you are still healing for another day or so, I will talk to the others to see if they can think of some way for you to repay us. Is there anything else you would like me to do for you?"

Between spoonfuls of the wonderful soup, I thought about her offer. Once again her tone suggested an invitation for something more than simple assistance. "The only other things I would like while I'm here are the saddlebags that were on the back of my bike. Would it be possible for you to…"

I suddenly felt extremely exhausted. It

88

seemed I was way too weary for the amount of energy expended since I woke up, even taking into account my injuries. I barely heard the spoon clatter into the empty bowl as I fell back against the pillow and fell hard asleep. I will never be sure if what I heard as I passed out was her actually speaking or just my imagination. "You sleep now; we will see if you can give us what we want."

It was dark outside when I woke up again. I certainly felt healthier and stronger this time than I had when I awoke with the sun shining in. At least this time I knew where I was and what was going on. Just like before, I turned and put my feet on the rug on the floor. This time, though, I was more gradual with my attempt to stand. There was no wave of weakness and black edges to my vision this time around. Despite being clear-headed and feeling quite capable, my legs were a little wobbly as I took a couple of tentative steps towards the door. I was almost close enough to reach out and touch the door when I saw the knob start to turn.

I took a careful step back as the door opened and the young woman from earlier came in without the soup bowl this time. She seemed a little surprised to see me awake and up but recovered quickly. "I see you are up again. I'm guessing your body needed a little more time to finish healing after your lunch this afternoon."

The wave of exhaustion that hit me after the soup didn't feel like anything I had felt before. Something was nagging at the back of my mind, but I had no reason to distrust this woman and her family. If they had truly wished to do me harm, they had more than enough chance to do so over the last couple of days. Still, I felt I should keep my guard up at least a little until I was sure of their intentions or able to leave.

"Are you hungry again? Would you like more soup?"

"No thank you. I'm still full enough after the last bowl you brought me. If you don't mind, could you tell me the way to the bathroom?"

"There is a bedpan under the foot of your bed. It's what we've been using for you since you arrived."

"It's ok, I would rather use an actual toilet if you have one. I need to move around some and walking would do me some good. Anything to help build my strength back up."

She came to my side and put an arm around my waist. "A little stroll down the hall can't hurt. Feel free to lean on me if you need to."

We walked out of the bedroom and turned down a narrow hallway. The handrail next to me led to a set of stairs going down. Glancing over the handrail I could only see one floor beneath me. I was in a two-story home. I still didn't know how many others lived here besides the young woman. She had mentioned sisters and an aunt, but I had yet to meet any other people.

I was able to walk down the hall on my own for the most part. We had to stop for a brief second before reaching the bathroom door. I still had plenty of breath, but my legs seemed weaker than they should have been with only a couple days off my feet. The young woman waited patiently outside the door while I took care of my business. We then slowly walked back to my room.

As I sat back on the bed I had been recovering in for the past two days, I decided to learn a little more about my situation. "Since we are both awake, do you mind if I ask a few questions?"

"Not at all. I might not be able to answer all of your questions, but I will tell you what I can."

"First things first, a simple introduction. I am Cade Van Housen. What is your name?"

"My name is Suzette. It was my grandmother's name."

"You mentioned your aunt finding me and your sisters helping to bring me here. How many people live here?"

"Right now it's my mother, my two sisters, and me living in this house. My aunts and their daughters live in the other two houses on the farmland. There are thirteen of us total."

Something unusual occurred to me. "You said your mother, sister, aunts, and their daughters. What about your father or uncles? Are there only women here?"

Suzette looked down at the floor, frowning for a second before raising her head and answering. "My father was killed in a logging accident a number of winters ago. One of my uncles went crazy and thought my other uncle was sleeping with his wife. Both uncles were killed in a nasty incident my family generally doesn't talk about."

"I'm sorry for asking."

"It's ok. I only heard about the incident. We don't speak of it for the sake of my cousins, especially since they are the ones that found the bodies."

"I understand. I will respect them and you by not mentioning it again." I paused then changed the subject. "Besides the herbs for your soup, what do you grow here? I grew up on my family's farm and I might be able to help once I'm healed."

"We grow a couple varieties of wheat to make our bread. We have a considerable vegetable garden with carrots, turnips, radishes, potatoes, and onions. We also maintain a couple of large fields for the goats and cattle that we use for milk and cheese."

"Besides the wheat, you only grow root vegetables? Is there any reason for that?"

"Each farm in the area specializes in one certain type of crop. It makes it easier to trade for what we need and minimizes the chances of disease spreading to other farms with similar plants. If one particular crop or farm is wiped out by insects or disease, we all lend a hand to help them out."

"It sounds like a good setup you have here. If you'd like, I will take a look at your crops when I can spend more time out of this bed. I am feeling a little tired and I think I saw you stifle a yawn yourself. Maybe we should call it a night for now and talk more in the morning."

Suzette agreed and got up to leave as I lay down under the covers. I could hear Suzette's footsteps as she walked down the hall in the opposite direction we had gone earlier. My room was apparently between hers and the stairs. I was not sure how I would use it, but this might be good information to keep in mind.

The next morning, I got out of bed and was able to walk without any problem. I grabbed my clothes from the chair and made certain the metal box I had been carrying was still in the inner pocket of my vest before putting anything on. Suzette had mentioned finding messages in my vest. Apparently she had felt the metal box was unimportant and left it alone. After getting dressed, I made my way to the head of the stairs. I noticed there was one more door on this floor besides my room, what I guessed was Suzette's room, and the bathroom. I could only guess it was another bedroom, probably belonging to one of Suzette's sisters.

As I neared the house's first floor, I could hear the faint sounds of conversation and utensils clattering against dinnerware. A group of people was having breakfast together. Although I couldn't hear the words, the chat sounded lively and friendly. I made my way towards the sounds emanating from what I assumed was the kitchen. The door opened before I got there and a younger version of Suzette walked through.

The younger sister saw me and turned back to the family. "Our guest is up and about."

An older woman's voice echoed from inside the kitchen. "By all means, invite the young man in. He's probably ready for a good solid meal. Caroline, would you please bring his saddlebags into the den while he eats?"

The young woman in the door—Caroline, I assumed—gestured for me to enter the kitchen and then disappeared on the mission to fetch my saddlebags. Suzette, her mother, and remaining sister were sitting at a table covered in breakfast foods. Suzette and Caroline definitely took after their mother when it came to looks. Their other sister had darker hair and her face had more of a square shape.

Pancakes were the main dish with buttered toast, small pieces of various melons, and milk to round out the meal. It all looked delicious. Suzette's mother introduced herself and the last sister I had yet to officially meet. "Good morning, Cade, and welcome to our table. I am Selena and the raven-haired beauty here is Louise. We are glad to see you up and about. Once you've had your fill, we will leave it up to you what you want to do next. You can inspect your bags, check the damage to your bike, or one of us can escort you around the farm for a bit."

"Selena, thank you and your daughters for your extreme hospitality to a simple clumsy messenger. After enjoying this food, I think I would like to check the contents of my saddlebags. I can get an inventory of parts for my bike before I see how much repair is really needed. I mentioned to Suzette that I would like to do something to repay you for your kindness. Have you come up with anything yet?"

"You don't need to worry yourself about payment for our assistance. We gave nothing that we don't have extra of. You have actually done us a small favor by consuming some things before they had a chance to spoil."

"I still need to give you some sort of compensation in exchange for the time I've spent in your home. At the very least I will take a look at your crops and give you any tips I may have learned. I can do that right after I inspect the damage to my bike since I will be outside anyway."

"We understand your desire to pay us for our hospitality. We will be happy to hear any advice you may have for us."

With that settled, we dove into the food enthusiastically. Caroline returned to the kitchen and enjoyed some breakfast as well. We moved to the den after satisfying our hungers. My saddlebags were on the floor next to an overstuffed chair. There were two other chairs and a large sofa, a matching set. There was also a piano with a bench next to it. I sat in the chair next to my saddlebags and lifted them into my lap so I could start sorting through the contents. Suzette and Louise each took a chair while their mother, Selena, stretched herself out on the couch. Caroline sat at the piano and began playing a tune. The music was soft and flowing. The other ladies soon picked up the song and hummed along with her. It was very relaxing to get down to work with such a beautiful chorus around me. They sang no words, but their hummed harmonies soared and fell, floating around each other and mixing together.

I reached deep into one of the saddlebags to check a hidden stash of food that was there. I had picked it up from a remote village about a day before my accident. They would make for a good lunch if I had to walk my bike to town to get parts. Three days later, the apples and bread should've still been good, however, when my hand entered the hidden pocket, I found the apple had rotted and become soft. The bread with it was hard as a rock. Stale beyond eating. Even the juices of the rotting apple should have kept the bread moist. There was no way this could have happened in only three days. It would take weeks or more for this to occur. Something was not right here.

Doing my best not to reveal my thoughts, I carefully replaced the spoiled food back into its hidden pocket. I pulled a spare tube for my tire and some tools from the saddlebag. "I hope I haven't been too much of a burden on all of you this past week."

Caroline turned to me without interrupting her piano playing. "It hasn't been that long really. Only a few days. Besides, you haven't been a burden on us at all. We have enjoyed having someone to take care of."

The other bag held only spare clothes and personal items. Since there wasn't anything in there that could help with repairs, I didn't bother to check it. "As much as I'm enjoying your an-gelic music, I must check on my bike now and see how much damage there is."

The song came to a beautiful end. Selena

spoke as her daughters got up from their seats. "Suzette will show you where your bike is. She can also help you find the tool shed in case you need something not in your handy bags there."

"It seems like I am constantly thanking you all." I stood up and slung my saddlebags over my shoulder with the tools in my other hand. Suzette moved next to me and wrapped her arms around my free arm. She led me to the front of the house and, together, we stepped outside. There was a crispness to the air as the chilly morning warmed up to become a comfortable afternoon. Suzette escorted me around to the side of the house without releasing my arm. Beyond a small grove of fruit trees, I could see a few fields for growing the wheat Suzette had mentioned. Between the house and the fruit grove was a considerable vegetable garden where I guessed the root vegetables were grown. Next to a large pile of firewood alongside the house was my bike.

The handlebars weren't bent like Suzette had said. They had just been knocked out of alignment, probably by my body flying over them. Some of the spokes in the front wheel were loose. I had what I needed to fix that much. It was the damage to the front wheel's rim that would be more difficult to repair. With a little work and a soft enough mallet, I could pound the rim back into its circular shape, but I had no way of balancing the tire and verifying how truly round the rim would be. Hopefully I could do enough to get into town and find someone with the equipment I needed.

Suzette let go of my arm as I started to work on the bike. I asked her if there was a chair or bench for me to sit on while I worked. I gave the brake handles a test squeeze and watched as the brake pads on each tire functioned properly. While Suzette was gone, I realigned the handlebars and ensured the bolt holding them in place wasn't damaged or stripped. The bolt was healthy and intact, just loosened a little bit. I had it tightened and the seat inspected by the time Suzette returned with a low wooden bench for me to use.

I sat down and flipped the bike over. Even though I had hit the tree in the front, I felt the need to check out all the moving parts of the bicycle. This included the pedals, chain, and rear derailleur, despite the fact they were far from the point of impact. Any problems with the chain or derailleur could be easily found and fixed before undertaking the difficult task of the front tire's rim. Suzette stood nearby and intently watched me work. I couldn't be sure if she was more interested in me or bicycle mechanics.

I had finished the basic maintenance and was checking the front forks for any sign of damage from the impact when Caroline showed up carrying a tray with some sliced bread, cheese, and pieces of meat. She also had three glasses of water and a pitcher in case someone wanted a refill. A light grumble in my stomach informed me I had been working on my repairs far longer than I thought. The three of us made sandwiches from the contents of the tray.

The young women sat on the ground across from me as I remained on the bench to eat. With my hands and mouth occupied with food, my mind began to argue with itself over the amount of time I'd been here. The food in my saddlebags told me I had been here a long time. Suzette and her family claimed it had only been a couple of days. If I had been here longer, why didn't I need to shave? Was there another way to verify what the date was?

I swallowed the last of my sandwich and looked around. "Would you ladies like to show me to the tool shed so I can see if you have anything that would allow me to straighten out my wheel?"

Suzette and Caroline glanced at each other and stood up together. Caroline answered with a grin and a sparkle in her eye, "Sure, if you would follow us, we can show you to the shed and help you find your tool."

With that, the beautiful young women each grabbed one of my arms and led me around the house towards a wooden shed in the distance. As we approached, I noticed the walls of the shed were thick and the door faced away from the house itself. The way Suzette and Caroline were smiling and walking, I had a feeling I wasn't the first male to be led to this shed and that the privacy it offered had been taken advantage of many times.

I entered the tool shed and noticed it was very clean and organized. It was also well lit by a skylight in the roof. There was a wide variety of hammers and mallets hanging on the back wall, so I stepped back there to see if they had what I needed.

I found a mallet I could use to straighten my wheel rim, took it from its hangers on the wall, and turned around to face the door. Suzette and Caroline were standing by the door in only their thin, silky slips, their dresses heaped on the floor beside them. Their dresses had fit loosely in a way that didn't flatter their female forms in the least. The shape of their figures were much more visible under the thin material of the slips. The thinness of the material and manner in which it moved made it clear that neither woman was wearing anything underneath their slips. The women sauntered in my direction with a glint in their eyes and a sway in their hips.

When they reached me, each woman started caressing my arms and pressing their scantily clad bodies against me. "Our mother doesn't usually let us play with our guests. As Louisa is the oldest, that is a privilege given to her. It was confirmed last week she is with child, so you become our toy today."

They started kissing my neck and cheeks. Their hands slipped under my shirt and were caressing my stomach and chest. My body was reacting to what they were doing. Unfortunately, my mind would not allow me to accept and enjoy the pleasures they were offering. I had to move on and I still wasn't too sure about trusting them since they had probably lied to me about how long I had been here. Something in my gut told me that I should not let these ladies get what they wanted, regardless of how much I would enjoy it.

"Ladies, you are very lovely. I am very, VERY tempted to accept your wonderful offer. I am certain all three of us would enjoy it. However, I have an important delivery I must complete. I'm sure we would all enjoy playing together, but I have to decline."

The sisters put on the most pitiful looks they could. They reminded me of sad little puppies missing a favorite toy. My regret at having to turn them down increased exponentially. I extricated myself from them and slowly walked out of the tool shed. I paused for a second when they started talking behind me, still in their seductive, breathy voices.

"Suzette, it looks like he isn't interested. Maybe we came on a little strong and are making him nervous. He might not even have been with a woman before. Perhaps we could show him a thing or two about giving pleasure and then let him join us."

Despite the fact I had started walking away, I was still close enough to hear their positions change. I could make out the soft sounds of the fabric of their slips being shifted across skin as they wrapped their arms around each other and started caressing each other's body.

"That might be it, Caroline, or it could be that he isn't interested in women at all. He might be more interested in playing if Father or one of our uncles was still around." Suzette's voice had a teasing edge to it.

I spoke in a flat voice loud enough for them to hear without turning around. "When it comes to pleasures of the flesh, I do prefer and enjoy the company of women. My partners have never said anything about a lack of satisfaction. Right now though, I have a different set of priorities. The package I am delivering is very important and must reach its destination. If I make it back this way again, I will most certainly enjoy playing with you until we are all satisfied and exhausted."

Once I was done speaking, I continued walking. There was no other sound or reaction from the women behind me. After taking a couple of steps around the shed, I was out of view from inside so I stopped and leaned against the exterior wall for a minute. I had to catch my breath and give my physical reaction to the sisters' attempts to seduce me a chance to settle back down.

I let out a soft sigh as I heard Caroline and Suzette pick up their dresses and start to put them back on. They didn't know I was still close enough to hear them as they started speaking in their every day, non-seductive voices again. "Well, Caroline, we tried it the easy way. Why don't you tell Mother what happened and she can figure out how to get what we need. I will see if I can't convince him to stay one more night."

I stood up and took long strides to get away from the tool shed before the sisters could emerge and catch me overhearing their strange conversation. I kept up my lengthy steps in order to reach my inverted bike quickly and get back to work well ahead of Caroline and Suzette.

I had removed the front tire from my bike by the time the sisters caught up to me. Caroline picked up the empty food tray she had brought our lunch out on and carried it back inside. Suzette settled herself in to watch me finish my repairs. At least I supposed that's what she was doing. Now though, she seemed less interested in my actions and the mechanics of the bike than she was before my reluctant refusal in the tool shed.

The sun moved across the sky quickly as I

worked hard to straighten the considerable dent in my front tire's rim. I was able to use the rubber mallet to get the shape to a near perfect circle again. It was visibly round, however, slight differences in the adjustments of the spokes as I re-installed them indicated that it was not quite perfect. It could still be ridden on, but I would need to get it checked and adjusted as quickly as possible. At least before I run into any more rough roads or trees lying across the pavement again.

Louisa made an appearance just as I was re-mounting the repaired wheel in its place on my bike. "Dinner is almost ready. It will be served in the formal dining room. Suzette, would you please escort our guest to the downstairs wash-room and then lead him to dinner?"

"I will, sister," Suzette agreed. She then looked at me to see if I was ready to go.

I tightened the bolts on my front tire and gave it a quick test before standing up and brushing my hands on my pants. "I've done as much here as I can. As long as I'm not imposing on anyone, I guess one more meal before I get back on the road would be ok. However, I must leave after the meal, while there is still some daylight left."

Suzette looked down at the ground as she stood up. "If that is what you wish, then we won't force you to stay any longer. You are healed and your bicycle is repaired. You can leave any time you want."

The three of us walked back into the house. Louisa went one direction while Suzette led me to a fine bathroom on the ground floor. It was much more elaborate than the simple one I had used on the second floor. There were two sinks beneath a large wall mirror. Across from them was a large round tub that could easily fit two people. In the corner sat a basic toilet with a fancy gold flushing handle. Since I didn't spend any length of time in one place, all of the decorations seemed wasteful to me, although I could understand how someone that spends their entire life in one place might like to see some variety.

Suzette and I washed our hands at the same time. I took extra care to make sure to get all of the grit and grime from repairing my bike off my hands. With the exception of the cheese soup, all of the foods I had seen were eaten by hand. I wanted to both show respect to my hosts and taste the full flavors of the food by not contaminating it with dirt from my hands. We dried our hands on separate towels hung on a rack by the tub. She then led me to the formal dining room. While remaining next to me, she seemed distant.

As we approached the dining room, it became clear which way we would need to go. I could have found it myself by following the aromas of a delicious meal drifting down the hallway. Suzette opened the door and gestured for me to precede her into the room. Everyone in the room was dressed simply. The elaborate decor of the room made it appear the clothing we all wore was even more simple and basic. A large rug with a square pattern covered the majority of the floor space. In the middle of the room was a long table that could easily hold ten diners. The five of us eating today would have more than enough room. The walls were covered in dark wood. Brightening the walls were fine landscape paintings in golden frames. All of the light in the room was provided by candles in a chandelier above the table and small candelabra at each end. The chandelier candles each had a glass cover that kept the flame steady and refracted the light, diffusing it around the room.

On the table was a set of fine china and elaborate silver utensils. The food had already been served and was steaming on the plates. The meal consisted of a large grilled piece of meat with carrots and cucumber slices on it, pasta in a creamy white sauce, and a mixture of peas and baby onions. Also at each seat were two crystal glasses. One was filled with water and the other appeared to contain a lightly colored fruit juice. I hadn't realized how hungry I was until I saw the food served up and ready to be eaten.

Everyone else was already at their seats when Suzette stepped into the room behind me. Selena sat at one end of the table, her presence making it the head of the table. Louisa was seated next to an empty chair on the near side of the table and Caroline was alone on the far side. The empty seats were pulled away from the table so that people could easily seat themselves without disturbing another diner.

Selena gestured to the seat next to Louisa. "Cade, please have a seat."

I sat down and waited for the others to start eating.

"Before we partake of this exceptional meal, I feel I should apologize to you, Cade," Selena continued. "Caroline and Suzette were too forward this afternoon. If they made you feel uncomfortable, it reflects poorly on all of us. Please, do not judge us based on their overzealousness today."

I looked across the table at Caroline and Suzette and gave them a friendly grin. "It's understandable, Selena. Everyone has certain urges and physical needs. There are also types of affection that can't be properly provided by members of the same family. I can't imagine you get many visitors here, so a little forwardness makes sense."

Selena picked up her fork and aimed it at the pasta on her plate. "I am glad you are so understanding. Now, let us all enjoy our meals."

We all grabbed our knives and forks and dug into the food on our plates. The sauce on the pasta was creamy. A sip of the fruit juice told me it was apple with a hint of cinnamon. I had always liked the contrasting flavors of baby onions and sweet peas. The ones on my plate had been cooked to perfection. The carrots and cucumbers had been grilled with the meat so they had a hint of its flavor as well as their own. The herbs and spices on the meat gave it a flavor that was unique but a little familiar. It was after my third bite that I realized the meat had been flavored with the same herbs used in the soup Suzette had given me shortly after I woke up. They worked equally well with the meat as in the soup.

I sampled each of the foods before really digging in to one in particular. Most of the pasta and all of the peas were gone when I decided to go after the meat and its carrots and cucumbers. Every few bites were washed down with occasional sips of the apple juice. Louisa had a pitcher close at hand to keep my glass from becoming completely empty. Most of the meat was gone when I was hit with a strong wave of exhaustion. It was just like the sudden sapping of my energy I had felt after the bowl of soup Suzette brought me when I first woke up. I hadn't exerted myself enough today to be experiencing this much of a lack of energy. I didn't have enough in me to get up from my chair. It was all I could do to look pleadingly at each of the female faces at the table around me before a growing blackness started filling my vision. The only place I could go was down and I was completely unconscious before my head hit the table in front of me.

All I could see was darkness. My other senses were working, if only barely. Faint voices were coming from all around me. I am pretty sure they were the voices of the women of the house. I was unable to make out what they were saying, despite the fact it seemed as though they were right next to me. I could feel a slight pressure from the back of my head, all the way down my body, to the backs of my heels. It took me a minute to realize it was because I was no longer in my chair, but lying down on something soft. The air in the room was a little cool on my skin. There was no reason for me to be this chilled, unless my clothes had been removed before I was placed on whatever was underneath me. I tried to move my arms and hands to verify my naked condition, but they didn't seem to respond. I wasn't able to move any parts of my body. There was a growing sensation inside me that felt like a pressure building. It wasn't unpleasant and I felt like I should be doing something more to savor the building of this pressure and enjoy its release.

A loud moan escaped my body as the pressure suddenly released and I realized exactly what it was. I was having an orgasm. My eyes suddenly snapped open and I was just able to raise my head enough to see what was happening. I was lying on the couch in the den where I had been serenaded earlier. Suzette was kneeling next to me at my waist, carefully collecting the fluid pulsing from my erect member in a glass held in one hand. My member itself was in her other hand. Her sisters were lounging in the chairs of the room. Selena was nowhere in sight. Louisa noticed my head moving as I did what I could to take in my surroundings.

"I told you the sedative wasn't balanced right. He's awake. Caroline, would you please go get Mother and let her know he has woken?" Louisa got up walked over to a side table and poured a glass of water. She set it next to the couch near my head. "You will need this in a minute. You can have it when you are mobile enough to grab it for yourself."

Suzette finished her task and sealed the glass that now contained my seed. She covered my naked body with a blanket. I shivered despite now being warm. Selena entered with a demure Caroline behind her. Selena took a seat in one chair and Louisa in another. Caroline sat down on the floor between the chairs and the couch, her dress becoming a circle on the rug beneath her. Suzette carried the glass jar out of the room as though it contained the crown jewels.

Whatever they had given me was weakening,

but still rather effective. I worked to turn my head in Selena's direction and barely uttered a single word, "Why?"

"The answer is both simple and complicated. I will try to keep it brief for you. We live a simple life of just us females. We have since the Exodus. Our family has been operating this farmland since generations before that. Besides farming, we also excelled at animal husbandry. There is a functioning lab in the basement that was used for combining the sperm of a herd's top males with the eggs of superior females without the risky business of actually breeding the pair. We could selectively nurture and implant the embryos for size, disease resistance, and gender. It didn't take much of a modification to adjust the lab's equipment for humans. Now we take the seed from ideal male specimens such as yourself, check them for a number of genetic diseases and conditions, select only the sperm containing the X chromosome, and fertilize our own eggs that we have stored. We prefer the 'extraction' process to be voluntary, but you refused to cooperate."

Despite my body's weakness, my mind was still sharp and functioning properly. While I could understand the how of what they were doing, the exact why still eluded me. Of all the questions running around my head, there were only two I needed an answer to. I barely croaked the first one, "What...you...give...me?"

Selena looked me over carefully before answering. "You are wondering what we slipped into your food to put you in this condition? It's a blend of sedative and paralytic herbs that my grandmother came up with. Mixed correctly and fully consumed, it can knock a person out and keep them absolutely still for hours. It is usually effective long enough for us to accomplish what we need to on those rare occasions we must take matters into our own hands to get what we need. I'm not sure if you have built up a tolerance from the soups we've been feeding you, or the dose wasn't right because you didn't eat all of the meat before it took effect."

That explained so many of the comments I had heard during my time here. It also went a long way towards explaining the aggressive actions of Caroline and Suzette in the tool shed. There was only one thing I really wanted to know. Their herbal sedative had worn off enough I could speak clearly and move my fingers and toes.

"How long have I been here?"

"When Suzette found you awake, she gave you the impression you had been in our care for only a couple of days. In all honesty, since there is nothing you can do to us at this point, you have been here for about three weeks. Your injuries combined with the sedatives in the soup kept you in a deep enough sleep for your body to do most of the healing by itself. We had discussed collecting a sperm sample from you then. It was determined that the increase in your blood pressure that an orgasm induces might not be good for your health considering the head injuries. Allowing you to waken on your own also let us gather more information regarding your general health."

I wasn't exactly happy about what they had done. The anger raging inside me had no physical way to express itself or be vented. If I had been physically able, I would have gotten up and left immediately. Even though it was the middle of the night, I would have gladly hit the road and ridden my bike as far from this place as I could. As it was, it would be best if I waited until the morning. I wanted to be sure the sedative and paralytic herbs would be out of my system so riding quickly to the next town would be safer.

I couldn't exactly report what Selena, her daughters, and the extended family were doing to male visitors. There was no real law prohibiting the extraction of sperm samples, as long as surgery wasn't performed on the subject. It hadn't occurred to anyone to ban pleasurably stimulating an unconscious subject until nature took its course and the sample was produced. No physical harm meant no legal issues to consider. Besides, even in the world that existed in these times after the Exodus, there were still some things an official wouldn't believe.

I took in a deep breath and let out a sigh of resignation. "Selena, I guess you and your daughters now have what you need in exchange for taking care of me. I hope you raise the granddaughter my seed produces well and she is healthy and strong. Since I imagine I will be recovered from the effects of your drug in a few hours, I will be leaving promptly at sunrise. No offense intended, but I won't be taking any supplies with me from here."

"We are not offended. I thought you might want some food to take with you, so I prepared a traveling bag. Caroline can take it with her the day after tomorrow when she takes some extra vegetables to market in the next town down the hill. As for the child, we take very good care of new daughters. We are, in our own way, modern 'Amazons' and ensure the health and strength of our own. Be quite assured, if you return and try to get your child, you will be unable to do so and there is nothing anyone else can do to help you."

If I had volunteered and accepted the offering of Suzette and Caroline earlier, I may have considered returning for my child. Since my seed had been stolen from me, I felt no attachment to the mother and would probably end up resenting the child because of it. In the coming days, I would do my best to forget this entire incident.

The only reminders I would have were the marks on my maps to avoid the area.

My body was still mostly paralyzed so there was nothing else I could do. I rolled my head away from Selena and closed my eyes in an attempt to get some natural sleep. I lay there slowly feeling my body return to me as I gradually fell asleep. The couch wasn't the most comfortable of sleeping surfaces, but I had rested on worse. At least my minimal ability to move would prevent me from falling to the floor during the remainder of the night. The following morning, I woke up to a silent house. Either I had risen before anyone else, or the others had left the house before I had finished sleeping. Regardless of the reason, I was more than happy to leave without encountering any of the women that lived here. With the questionable morals of the mother and daughters living here, I double-checked the metal box that was my primary reason for my trip. There were some minute scratches near the latch. It looked like someone had tried to force the box open and failed.

HAZARDS

Rain was falling lightly as I pedaled down the road. The usual sounds of my tires on the road had an additional tone as water squished out from between the treads. Drops were pattering against the few remaining the leaves on the trees. The wind was mostly calm so the drops were falling almost straight down. I was still getting soaked, but most of the water was staying out of my eyes. Visibility was only impeded by the small amount of sunlight the clouds let through and the stream of water falling in front of me.

It was not surprising that at first I didn't see the body in the road ahead of me. I was nearly on top of it before I could even identify the body as human. The falling rain had washed away any signs of blood, removing any chance for me to tell if he had been lying there for minutes or hours. The only things I could obviously tell were that he was a fellow messenger and that he was dead. He wasn't wearing a multi-pocketed vest like mine but instead, carried a large messenger bag. The bag was more popular with most messengers, but I felt it would interfere with my legs as I pedaled my bicycle. Out of respect for the deceased, I moved the body off the road and placed him under as much cover amongst the trees as I could, given the mud and my lack of a shovel.

I picked up the messenger bag with the intent of looking through it later. I didn't want to open it in the rainstorm and risk ruining any letters that might be inside. I put the messenger bag inside one of my saddlebags and continued down the road. I was pretty certain there was a small town ahead that would have a few places to find protection from the weather.

The rain lightened up but didn't stop completely as I crested a hill and spotted the town I was expecting nestled in a small valley. Trees surrounded the town's buildings and were scattered alongside the streets. It was a very peaceful town in a serene environment. I sincerely hoped nobody in this quiet town had known the deceased messenger personally. Since I had found the body, I was obligated to inform the next of kin if possible. It was a duty that I would prefer to avoid, but would perform if necessary.

I rolled down the hill and into town as the rain finally stopped. I spotted a couple of crude handmade signs that pointed to City Hall. I was hopeful I could find someone there to inform about the dead messenger. Entering City Hall, I saw there were no new messages waiting to be sent out. The message board was clearly displayed, but the boxes were all empty. The messenger that had passed away on the road outside of town must have been here recently.

The interior walls of City Hall were decorative wood panels. Plants were artfully placed in the corners of the room. The floor was covered with colored ceramic tiles laid out in an old fashioned pattern. This city hall was most likely built long before the Exodus caused a shortage in the manufacturing of luxury materials. There were two doors leading out of the entry hall. One was labeled "Kitchen," the other "Conference Room." I wondered how much use these rooms got in the modern days.

I opened the satchel and looked through the contents. There was a decent collection of maps that I added to my own. One map showed the immediate area. The only notation was a hastily scrawled word. It said "Hunters" in bold letters across this valley. I figured the notation meant the residents hunted for their food instead of farming. It gave me a good idea of what kind of food to expect in trade for making a delivery.

The messenger bag also contained a number of envelopes. Most were regular envelopes that could still be found in stores. There were a couple of handmade envelopes, one of which stood out. It was as red as fresh-flowing blood. The edges were trimmed in the gold of the sun as it rose above the horizon. A blob of light blue wax with an ornate symbol pressed into it sealed the back of the envelope. I had never seen anything so elaborate. This was very clearly an important message in the sender's mind. I placed it with the other messages going east. I would have to make sure I came through this town again. If the message was still there, I would carry it myself and see if the recipient felt as though the message was worth the dressing it was wrapped in.

Someone entered the lobby as I finished placing the messages in the slots of the message board. I placed the red envelope in a slot by itself and turned to see who was here with me. It was an older man with short, white hair and a full beard. His beard had a few brown spots in it. From this distance, however, I couldn't tell if the spots were natural coloring, food, or dirt. He wore a simple shirt and pair of pants. There seemed to be similar spots on his clothes. This was clearly someone that was used to hard work. Either that, or he had gotten unlucky near a mud puddle formed by the recent rains.

"Welcome to Rushton. I am the mayor, Gene. It seems you have brought us a significant amount of mail today. Do you mind if I ask where it is all from?"

"Hello, Gene, I'm Cade. Unfortunately, this mail is bound for other areas. I found another messenger dead just outside of your town. These are what he was carrying east. I have an important delivery I must make west, otherwise I would take them myself."

"We thank you for bringing our important messages back to us. Communication between distant family members and communities is so difficult and unreliable. Bringing these messages back to us will, at the least, give us the assurance that they aren't lost out there somewhere."

"Once my delivery is done, I will come back this way and deliver any messages that are still remaining."

"I thank you for that. We get messengers so frequently, I doubt these same messages will be there. You will most likely find a different set waiting for your arrival. There is no way we can truly show our appreciation for the service you messengers provide."

"It is a life we choose, knowing that the traveling will be rough and good meals may be few and far between. We do it so those that must work hard to provide for their families don't need to leave them to spread good news and bad. Roads are safe because the only ones traveling them the majority of the time, are those of us who have what we need."

I turned and started to make my way to the door. With the storm gone, I felt I should get some more miles behind me before settling down for the night. Try to make up for time and distance lost during the falling rain. Gene stopped me before I could make it out the door.

"Please. I have a request to make of you. Can you wait a minute while I get something from my office, then carry it west for me?" He stepped around me and entered a side door that led off the lobby. The door had a false panel on it that exactly matched the wall panels around the room. After a minute, he emerged carrying a dark blue envelope decorated in a similar manner as the red one I had found in the dead messenger's satchel. The gold edging was just as elaborate. The differences were the color of the envelope itself and the wax stamp that sealed it closed.

"Where is this message going?" I held my hand out and the mayor placed the elaborate envelope carefully in it.

"The main highway leading out of town will take you directly to the town of Corrington. This message is for the wife of the mayor there. I would consider it an extra favor if you could deliver it to her by hand."

I placed the thick envelope in one of the pockets of my vest. It would be safe there for the duration of my ride to Corrington. Reviewing my maps, I saw the route would be easy enough and allow me to continue directly on my main delivery mission. "Do you happen to have any dried fruit or some bread for me to take along? In exchange for delivering such an important message, of course."

"Of course. Just give me a moment and I will bring you something to take along." Gene walked across the lobby and stepped through the door marked "Kitchen." He was gone less than a second; the sound of the door had barely ceased echoing, before he reemerged with a small sack in his hand. "There are a couple of apples, some sourdough bread, and a small container of honey in here. I hope that is payment enough for your effort."

I smiled as I took the bag from him, trusting his list of contents and not looking inside. "That is more than enough. Thank you very much."

With his well wishes, I walked out of City Hall and grabbed my bike where I had left it by the door. I put the sack of food in the saddlebag with the other supplies I had. My stock of food was running low. This sack wouldn't add much to it, but it would get me through the day without depleting my already dwindling supply of food on hand.

I mounted my bike and started riding out of the cozy little town. The rain was gone and the clouds were clearing. The sun was emerging to dry up the puddles and mud. What remained of the day would be wonderful for riding in. The wind seemed to be coming from behind me, giving me a good sign as it sped me along my way.

The road climbed the valley between the hills and away from the town of Rushton. The ground leveled out just after the peak of the hill and led into some scattered trees. Broken patches of sunlight littered the pavement. The view ahead of me seemed to be improving by the second. The air was clean and crisp.

As I rode between the trees, I noticed a sudden odd smell on the wind, a slight hint of something unclean, a combined odor of old sweat and rancid fruit, but only when drafts shifted from the right direction behind me. Subtly glancing around, I happened to catch a shadow move between the trees behind me to my right. Another one ahead of me to my left shifted in a manner that no amount of wind could cause. In anticipation of some trouble, I shifted my hand close to my holstered shotgun. I knew it was loaded and ready to fire. Eight rounds were loaded and I had a dozen more clipped to the stock and ready. I also had a box of rounds in my saddlebags, but they would be useless in an emergency situation.

More shadows moved ahead of me. I was withdrawing my shotgun with one hand and readying to fire it before the first shadow broke from the trees ahead of me and formed into a very dirty man. He was standing in the middle of the road holding a large knife. While it looked like he was expecting me, he seemed a little surprised at my awareness of him. I stretched my arm out and aimed the shotgun at him while pedaling harder to accelerate. I had plenty of road on each side of me to veer out of his line of fire if he drew a gun.

Another person emerged from the opposite side of the road. This one appeared to be a woman, just as dirty as the man already facing me. I quickly put my feet down and stopped my bike. I straddled my bike, keeping it standing with my legs. I now held the shotgun with both hands and kept it ready to fire. I glanced behind me to see if I could spot a way to back out of the ambush, but two more grimy individuals were now standing on the road in my previous path. It was becoming clear that I had ridden myself into a situation similar to the one faced by the unfortunate messenger I had come across earlier.

I had an odd feeling that this was not the first time these folks had done this. The only question on my mind was why weren't they advancing. Even with my shotgun, I knew I wasn't that menacing a figure to four assailants. All four figures were keeping their distance from me. With solid rounds in my shotgun, I could easily take two or three of them out before any of them got close enough to hurt me. Assuming none of them was armed with more than a knife or sword anyway. Unfortunately, I only had bird shot on me. I had figured that any situation calling for me to fire would require a larger area of damage for optimal effect. Four aggressors in a wide area around me was something I didn't think I would ever be facing.

Keeping my head turning back and forth, I was able to keep an eye on all four attackers. They still weren't coming any closer to me, even when I wasn't looking directly at one of them. Without taking my eyes off of them or releasing my shotgun, I used my foot to lower the kickstand of my bike. I carefully dismounted and stood next to it. I could move more freely now if I had to.

I started swinging my gun from person to person as I studied the first person that had emerged from the trees. Even though they were close enough to be heard with my usual voice, I yelled to be heard more clearly. "Who are you? What do you want?"

There was no response. They didn't even acknowledge that I had spoken at all. I took two steps forward. The pair in front of me backed away two steps. Glancing around, I saw the two people behind me had stepped forward, keeping the exact same distance from me they had before. I turned around and raised my shotgun. Aiming it at one of the aggressors that had been behind me, I took the two steps back to stand next to my bicycle. The person I was aiming at didn't move, but the other person blocking my route back to town backed away. I glanced at the other pair and they were still as far from me as they had been. Looking to the person staring down my shotgun's barrel I noticed he had stepped back when my eyes weren't on him. Everyone was now back into the positions they had started this whole charade in.

I urgently needed to get on my way and my patience with these four was wearing thin. However, they hadn't done anything overtly aggressive so I couldn't bring myself to shoot any of them, at least not yet. I was tempted to remount my bike and start riding again, but wasn't really sure if the man and woman in front of me wielded their knives well enough to hit a moving target. There were too many unknowns for me to be forward in this situation. If I only knew what they were all waiting for, I would at least have a better idea if I should wait with them or go ahead and charge my way past.

I was satisfied to sit here and wait with these four until I saw more shadows move amongst the trees. The four people I was facing were waiting for reinforcements. There was no way for me to know how many more people were coming to attack me here on the road. My only option was to charge ahead with my shotgun firing and hope no more had arrived to block me in again. With an unknown number of people coming to help those already around me, I had to move fast before I didn't have enough ammunition readily available to get away.

I quickly hopped back onto my bike and charged at the guy in front of me to my right. I kept my shotgun trained on him. I could see the panic starting to form on his face as he realized there was no way he could avoid both me and the pending shotgun blast. Just before I reached him I suddenly veered to my left and fired at the woman there. She seemed to be falling in slow motion as I turned to retrain myself back on the man. I failed to notice the thin string hanging between them until it was too late.

If both of the people had been standing, the string would have cut right across my chest and knocked me flat onto the pavement. Since the woman was falling with the smoke of my shotgun blast still hanging in the air, the string had been lowered and had some slack to it. There was still enough tension for the string to catch in my handlebars and cause me to lose some control. Riding with one hand holding my shotgun wasn't enough for me to avoid a fall. Fortunately, the maneuvers to fire at the woman and re-target the man had slowed me down enough to keep from having a major fall. I ended up on the ground with my bike falling near me. After a quick roll, I lay on my back and sighted my shotgun back at the man near me before he could take advantage of my prone position.

The grungy man that had been in front of me

came to a quick stop once he saw the barrel of my shotgun aimed in his direction once again. There was a look of near eagerness on his rough face and his knife was held high, ready to strike me as I lay on the ground. I glanced at the other two attackers without taking my eyes completely off of the knife wielder before me. They had gotten closer while I was falling, but stopped while still at a safe distance from me. Two more people joined them from between the trees while I looked. These two were even dirtier than the three I was already facing. If more people appeared, I would have enough extra shells to handle them, but reloading time might be hard to come by.

I carefully stood up and took a step back so I could keep all five of them in my view while my shotgun was still trained on the closest. I asked earlier, but felt maybe the new arrivals might have an answer. "Ok, I'm going to ask this one more time. Who are you and what do you want?"

"You have been more of a challenge than some of the others that have come through our town. You certainly got further up the road than we expected. You are also much better armed than other messengers. You have given us a decent hunt." The voice saying this was familiar. I was able to identify exactly who it was when the owner walked out from between the trees. It was Gene, the mayor of Rushton. Unlike the others, he was armed with more than a knife. He had a pistol in his hand and two more holstered on his belt. The gun in his hand was aimed at me.

"So you and your friends here hunt people that travel through your town? It seems to me that would deter repeat visitors."

"We don't hunt all visitors. Just messengers like you. Whichever one of us manages to get our hands on that special envelope I gave you gets an extra meat ration. It's just too bad we weren't able to find the red one the last yutz had. The storm rolled in and the rain was making it hard to see. Besides, I was getting wet and the hunt hadn't required enough energy to warrant the extra ration."

"So you just hunt messengers. You kill those that have no family and have dedicated themselves to selflessly carrying letters for others. How is it you can do such a thing?"

"We enjoy hunting people. Messengers are the best prey because of the minimal chance of retribution. No family to seek vengeance. No inquisitive friends to come poking into our business. They aren't tradesman so their travel routes aren't known in advance. Messengers move randomly and aren't expected anywhere at a specific time. Nobody misses a messenger if they disappear."

"So you hunt and kill us because you don't have to worry about someone else coming along to search for us and hunting you back. You can be certain I will be passing this information along to other messengers and posting this town's position on all the messenger boards I come across."

"You are assuming an awful lot. Before you can do any of that, you have to get out of here alive. That is something no other messenger has been able to do."

Five enemies around me plus Gene and seven rounds still ready to fire in my shotgun. The odds weren't exactly in my favor, but I had enough ammunition to even things up a little. I just had to keep a close eye on Gene since he was the only other person with firearms. Even if I ran out of shots, I could fend off those wielding the knives by using my shotgun as a club in hand-to-hand combat.

I just had to choose my targets carefully here at the start of the conflict. If I could get two or more of them in a group, I could injure several with a shot or two. The best I could hope for was causing enough severe injuries to take someone out of commission so I wouldn't have to worry about them. I might be able to use their little herding method from earlier against them.

I stepped back and moved to one side of the road. This would keep everyone in my line of fire. Hopefully they would bunch to one side of the road in order to keep their relative distance from me. Then I could use the rushing attack tactic on foot that I used from my bike on the poor deceased woman.

As I had expected, the group bunched up on one side of the road. They weren't as tightly grouped as I would have preferred, but it was still a close enough gathering for me to do some damage with minimal ammunition expended. Gene was in the middle of the pack. I could use his own companions to block his line of fire if I moved just a little bit to my left.

I rushed at the pack of attackers, angling to my right a little. I would become a better target for Gene, but I was planning on him taking a shot at me before I could get too close. If my luck held, he would do me a favor and injure or kill one of his fellow hunters for me. Gene raised his gun and started to take aim. If he was going to fall for my trick, I had to do it now.

Without breaking my stride I suddenly changed my path to sharply angle back to my left. I quickly came within a couple of feet of the first attacker. I fired a shot from my hip and hit him in the stomach. I was close enough that I was bound to hit him somewhere. My sudden change in direction and the boom of my shotgun was enough to cause Gene to pull his own trigger. His attention was so intently focused on me that he failed to notice that another of his companions was in his line of fire. The bullet left the pistol's chamber and struck one of his associates in the back of the shoulder. He dropped his knife and fell to the ground, clutching his wounded shoulder and cursing Gene for his error.

I stepped over the fallen man I had shot and around the one Gene had dropped without losing any speed. Dropping to my knees I was able to slide to a quick halt right before Gene. He was too startled by his accidental shooting of one of his own men to be able to aim his pistol back on me. He suddenly found himself standing still with me on my knees before him. My shotgun was aimed directly at his swollen stomach, the end of the barrel mere inches from his flesh.

I didn't take my eyes off of Gene at all as I yelled a threat to his three remaining companions. "One slight twitch from any of you and your mayor here will have a whole new collection of holes in his stomach."

The others stood completely still. It looked like they were too afraid to put their knives back in their sheaths for fear the motion would cause me to shoot their mayor and lead hunter. Gene was also keeping as still as stone in order to not get himself perforated. His pistol was still aimed where I was before I dropped to my knees and slid to a stop. Keeping my trigger finger ready on my shotgun, I reached up and pulled the pistols from the holsters on his belt. I tucked each pistol into the back of the waistband of my pants. Before he had a chance to move and aim his remaining pistol at me, I reached further up and pulled it from his grasp. This one I tossed into the woods.

I felt a little better with Gene now disarmed and nobody else willing to move. I stood and backed up, keeping my shotgun aimed at Gene. As I spoke, I stepped back until I was standing next to the spot where my bike had fallen. "What will it take to make you stop attacking messengers?"

Gene's voice was a lot less certain now than it had been before. His racing heart was returning to its normal pace as he answered my question. "Nothing will make us stop. There is nothing to entertain us. None of the towns around us are large enough to have what passes for Internet access. Television is nonexistent. Radio broadcasts are little more than farm reports. With no major government and political squabbling, even talk shows, as they exist, are no longer entertaining. Hunting people is how we relieve the boredom of our lives."

"So messengers have been dying to entertain you. This will end now." I had reached my bicycle. I leaned down and picked my bike up. I leaned it against my hip while I considered my options. I could leave here and do as I had mentioned earlier, flagging the area as a place to be avoided at all costs. Unfortunately, it would take

time for word to spread to others. In the meantime, others would die before word reached
them. The only way to stop this would be to
eliminate the leader of this little group. Killing
wasn't something I wanted to do or took pleasure
in. I had no problem firing in self-defense, but
shooting someone in cold blood was a different
matter entirely.

I put my shotgun back in its holster. Without
turning my back to the group of hunters, I slowly
got back on my bike. Gene decided to try and
push his luck and take advantage of his superior
numbers. With a single yell of "Attack" he made
my final decision for me. As the hunters started
to advance on me, I pulled one of Gene's pistols
from behind me and started firing. I kept myself
sighted on Gene as the pistol fired repeatedly.
Red holes appeared up Gene's body and he
started to fall. A look of pure shock crossed his
face as he fell back. The others stopped before I
could fire again and send them to join Gene in
the afterlife.

"Now that your leader is dead, you will stop
hunting messengers. As a people, we were given
a second chance when the meteor missed us.
Don't ruin it by continuing Gene's poor idea of
entertainment." With that final message, I turned
my bike around and started pedaling away from
the town of Rushton and its demented citizenry.
After covering a few miles, I tossed the pistol I

had nearly emptied at Gene into the trees. I slid the other into the holster by my handlebars that had been empty since I was first given my bike. After a moment's consideration I pulled the blue envelope Gene had given me earlier from my vest. I tossed it to join the nearly empty pistol in the bushes between the trees.

I reached the town of Corrington before nightfall. The town was empty. It appeared as though nobody had lived here since the Exodus. I took shelter in a vacant house for the night. Reaching into my saddlebag for some food, I found the bag Gene had given me back in his City Hall. It contained exactly what he told me: two apples, a small loaf of sourdough bread, and a ceramic container of honey. There was also one more thing he hadn't mentioned. It was a small electronic device. I could only guess that it was a transmitter and Gene had a receiver for it. Gifting past messengers with the food bag would make it easy to hunt them. They could then recover the device from their prey and put it into another bag for the next messenger. Taking a bite from the bread, I set the transmitter on the floor and smashed it with my boot.

DELIVERY

I climbed one more hill in the northern section of the former state of California. I could see a large building nestled against a lake amid the trees. The lab was located west of the town of Redding itself. I wasn't able to take the most direct route out of the town since the major highway had been damaged by forest fires and repeated mudslides over the last five decades. It was only possible for me to reach the lab by taking secondary roads and country trails. A helpful woman in Redding was familiar with the lab and was able to give me directions.

The building looked brand new. There were smaller buildings around it still under construction. There was much more activity than I had ever seen around the laboratory near my hometown. Even though I knew it was there, I touched the place on my vest where the box rested in my hidden pocket. The box was light enough I had hardly noticed it was there most of the time. I would still be glad to drop it off and maybe see what was inside of it. It would be nice to be able to more freely pick which directions I traveled and what destinations I carried messages to. However, I would miss having a long-term goal to reach, but now I would be able to take a more circuitous route or change my destination entirely on a whim.

First though, I had to finish this delivery. My final destination was so close I could see it, literally. I approached the area and saw some people moving about. Some were clearly laborers working on the buildings being constructed. Others wore lab coats so white they shined in the daylight. While the people weren't as active as ants in an anthill, there was quite a bit of activity.

I drew some attention as I rolled into the collection of buildings. People still moved about on their various activities, but many slowed down to see the man rolling amongst them on the silver bicycle. I made directly for the large laboratory building. I could see an entrance with a bicycle rack next to it. There were two bikes leaning there already. Neither seemed to be equipped like mine, but they were similarly built. I parked my bike with the others and walked to the door.

I couldn't find any way to open the door from my side. There was no knob to turn or handle to pull on. The door also lacked a push bar to press the door open with. I wondered if this lack of an opening mechanism was intentional or simply from the door being incomplete like the rest of the buildings in the area. Looking the door over,

I noticed a speaker next to the door with a small button under it. Rather than waiting an unknown amount of time until someone else opened the door, I pushed the button and waited for a response. After a minute of waiting without a response, I pushed it again. I was pressing it a third time when a frustrated voice finally came over the speaker.

"You too much of a fool to remember the procedure or just feeling like being a prankster?"

I spoke back to the speaker as I pushed the button again. "I'm sorry, this is my first time here. I have a package to be delivered here and have no idea how to get in."

The voice was much friendlier as it came over the speaker again. "Instructions should be on the sign to the left of the door. They will tell you how to get in."

I glanced to the left side of the door. There had been nothing there when I first walked up to the door, and that remained true now. I looked at the dirt near the door to make sure it hadn't fallen off. Pressing the button, I figured the speaker voice might want to know this. "There is no sign next to the door. It isn't on the ground either. Would it be possible for you to let me in so I can deliver this package?"

"Yeah. I'll let you in. Be careful, the door opens outward so don't stand too close. It will be dark inside, but the lights will come on once the door closes completely. I will meet you at the desk at the end of the hall and to the right."

The speaker clicked off and a buzz signaled the opening of the door. It swung far enough for me to grab the side of it and open it so I could enter the darkened building. As promised, as soon as the door clicked closed, the lights flickered on and lit my way down the stark white corridor. There were no doors off the hall that I could see, just a junction at the far end. The walls were plain as far as I could see. The floor was a smooth, reflective plastic tile that I had only seen worn and rotting in empty buildings.

I could hear the sounds of a voice echoing from the far end by the junction. I walked toward the voice and was able to make out exactly what was being said just over half of my way there. The mumbles were complaints about contractors, painters, and something about incorrect work orders. While I understood what he was saying, the content was still confusing to me. I saw the grumbling figure as I reached the end of the hall and looked right as instructed.

A man was sitting at a simple desk with a large pad of paper in the middle of it. Looking at it upside down I could see what looked like a list of names and numbers. Whoever was running this place certainly liked to keep track of who was coming and going. There was also a small speaker box with a button on it, similar to what was outside the door that had been opened for me. A second button stuck up from the top of the desk. This was probably the button that had opened the door for me. The small, balding man sitting at the desk making notes on a notepad looked up at me as I stepped up to the desk.

"You have a package to deliver?"

"Yes I do. I have brought it from Eastern Eddie." I started to reach into my vest's inner pocket to grab the small box when the guy's eyes lit up and his face filled with excitement.

"Eastern Eddie you say? We've been expecting something from him for some time." He shook his head at me as I reached out to hand him the box. "I don't have the key to open that. You need to take it to Professor Joe. He's down the hall behind me, third door on the left. Things are about to get very busy around here."

I walked around the desk and started down the hallway. Finding the door was easy enough. This time there was a handle. I pulled the door open. Inside was a room full of shelves with jars and beakers surrounding worktables covered in scattered papers and microscopes. One man was sitting on a tall stool with his back to me. He appeared to be studying whatever was in front of him very intently. At least until a light snore gave away the fact he wasn't studying, he was sleeping.

I let the door close on its own. The thud of

the door in the frame and click of the latch was enough to wake the gentleman without startling him off of his stool. I got a good look at him as he turned around to see who had intruded on his nap. He was completely bald and had a small white goatee. On his nose was perched a pair of wire rimmed glasses. They were low enough under his eyes to allow him to read through them and still look over them at whatever else was worth looking at. He had more of an athletic build than any other lab worker I had seen before. He greeted me with a voice as gentle as feather pillow.

"Welcome, young man. I guess I should thank you. If I'd slept in that position much longer, it would have been very difficult for me to get up with the knot that would have developed in my back." He rubbed some of the sleep from his eyes then looked at me over his glasses. "I know everyone that lives and works here and you don't seem familiar to me. Mind telling me who you are?"

I held the box out to the professor. "My name is Cade and I have a delivery from Eastern Eddie. Are you Professor Joe by any chance?"

The same look of excitement washed over the man's face that had struck the one at the desk earlier. This package from Eastern Eddie obviously meant quite a lot to these people. My curiosity over the contents was growing.

142

"I am Professor Joe. We have been waiting for that box you have right there. Its contents could mean more than you know for all of humanity. Those of us here on Earth as well as those that left in the Arks."

Professor Joe couldn't have known how much I desired to see exactly what I was holding. I was determined not to leave until I learned the full importance of the contents of the box I had carried across the entire country. If whatever it was had an effect on those that left during the Exodus, it had to be a powerful item indeed.

The Professor walked over to me and took the box in both hands. He carried it to a cabinet built into the wall. Professor Joe hadn't said I could stay as he opened the box, but he didn't ask me to leave either. Opening the cabinet, he took out a strange key. It had three sets of teeth on it that were spaced to fit exactly into the slots on the front of the box. Professor Joe glanced questioningly at me when he saw the scratches on the surface of the lock.

"I was laid up with injuries for a few days. My hostesses tried to open the box without my knowledge during my convalescence."

This answer seemed to satisfy the Professor. He slipped the strange key into the lock and gave it a lift rather than a turn. The top of the box popped up like the clown in a jack-in-the-box. Professor Joe opened the box the rest of the way.

A small object sat on a padded cushion in the middle of the box. It was plastic and a couple of inches long. There was a small metal slit at one end. Apparently Professor Joe was aware of my lack of knowledge regarding the small object without looking up from his inspection of it.

"It's called a USB or flash drive. They were very common as portable data storage devices before the Exodus. They are extremely rare now. We only use them for exchanging large data files between a handful of labs across the country. A flash drive is more durable and easier to encrypt than a disc. All the labs we communicate with have computers and are networked using the infrastructure of the old Internet. Now, let's go see what Eastern Eddie has to tell us."

Professor Joe set the box down on a nearby table and pulled the flash drive out of it. He carried it like it was a fragile egg with cracks already in the shell. He wanted to hold onto the device firmly enough that he didn't drop it, but not so hard as to break it. I followed him into another room with an aged computer sitting on an otherwise empty desk. I had seen pictures of computers before and was able to look one over in a large city library. The library computer was only operated one day a week and I had visited on the wrong date to be able to use it myself. The piece of electronic equipment before me was running and fully functional. What I was about to see was something that almost nobody on the planet saw anymore. Almost all of those with computer knowledge went on the Arks to keep complicated systems functioning. Those left behind were able to use computers for a few years until individual systems and large servers started breaking down. A rare few people were able to study manuals and schematics to get a single system running for an entire town. Apparently some laboratories also managed to keep a technician trained and on hand to maintain their computers for research and some communication.

Professor Joe inserted the metal end of the flash drive into a slot on the front of the computer's main box. With a couple of clicks he had access to the files on the drive. He maneuvered the cursor expertly and opened a program on the computer that could process the files he wanted. The professor opened the files in the program and a series of lines of text and numbers began filling the screen.

"The files you brought me are part of two different systems. One is the planned courses of the Arks that left during the Exodus combined with tracking data from the few functioning space telescopes. The other system is a powerful communications laser system. These files are the communications frequencies used by the Arks and the audio encoding subroutines. Once the compiler I have running is done with the data, programs, and processors, we will know exactly where each Ark is and how to reach out to it. We will be able to talk to them again after all these years."

I was feeling a mixture of confusion, excitement, and nervousness. "How exactly can you do that? Also, why would you want to talk to them?"

"This lab is electronically linked to a communications tower that was built on a nearby mountain. It was a critical component during the construction of the Arks themselves. It has its own power supply for the pulse laser it used to send messages relatively quickly and directly to the Arks. It also has a focused receiving system designed to get messages from distant planets. A remnant of the long extinct SETI program looking for other intelligent beings. We are using a laser communication system because it gets less interference than a radio signal and can be transmitted further without significant signal loss. The downside is we need to point the transmitter right at the Ark in order for them to receive the broadcast.

"We want to talk to the Arks in order to tell them the apocalypse they left to avoid never happened. We won't be asking them to come back to Earth, but would like them to know we are still here. We can also learn about their status and make sure no disaster has befallen any of them."

I was getting more excited as Professor Joe talked and I watched the compiler program fill the screen with more computer commands and data. "It all sounds like good news to me. Do you want me to carry mass messages out to Redding and other towns when you hear from the first Ark?"

There was a hint of concern on the Professor's face as he looked back at me. "I don't think that would be a good idea. When we were first looking for people to build our little community here, we asked if people would like to hear from the Arks some day. The majority of responses we got were negative. The people had grown to like the lives they had built here and were afraid the return of the Arks might mean a return to an existence they don't want. More than a handful of people threatened violence on anyone that did reach out to the Arks. That's why we have the security measures at the door, such as they are. We want to be safe and private until we know whether or not we can speak to the Arks and if a return is even possible."

The lack of an outer door handle on the building made a lot more sense to me now. They could let in only the people they knew would agree with their attempts and not those that might sabotage the equipment. Much of humanity had moved on since the time before the Exodus, but it appeared some would always feel they were the only ones with the right opinion and might get violent to defend that fact.

Professor Joe watched the computer work for another minute then stood up. "This is going to take a few hours to calculate. Would you like to get something to eat with me? We have quite a variety of fresh foods available if you'd like something a little different."

With my mind working on the possible ramifications of being able to talk with the Arks, I hadn't realized that I was hungry. Breakfast had been in Redding before the long ride out to the lab. I was curious where their fresh foods might come from. I hadn't seen any gardens in the area. Just a few buildings under construction and some domes on the outskirts of the cleared trees. Professor Joe led me to one of the domes. Underneath was a thriving vegetable garden. Each dome was a green house with enough ripening vegetables for the entire compound and some extra to sell at the market in Redding. The greenhouses were kept at different temperatures and light levels to simulate different parts of the growing season. This allowed the farmers of the compound to harvest their crops every couple of months regardless of the season in the outside world. It would be a real treat to be curled up by a warm fire during a winter chill and eat some fresh picked strawberries.

Professor Joe and I each got a plate of our choices of fruits and vegetables and a small bowl of a stew with meat from local wildlife. I didn't ask precisely what animals because my mind was occupied with thoughts of the possibility of the Arks returning. Many luxuries people enjoyed before the Exodus would return, but so would many of the issues that caused much suffering. A balance could be achieved if only some of the Arks came back. The problem would be deciding who to allow to return and how to ask some not to. Who should be allowed to make that decision anyway? It was becoming clearer to me why some people might get violent to prevent any kind of contact with the Arks in the first place.

I was so involved in my thoughts that I hardly noticed when Professor Joe started talking to me. "The computers will probably be compiling the programs for the rest of the day today and it will be all day tomorrow while we get the communications laser warmed up and calibrated. Since that is automatic, we can use the data from the telescopes and expected courses of the Arks to locate them in the skies. Would you like to stick around for a couple more days and be with us when we transmit the first signal, or do you have another important delivery to make?"

In order to complete this delivery as quickly as possible, I had picked up no more messages the last few days of my journey. I had considered seeing what messages might be taken out of Redding when I left the laboratory facilities, but I could wait a few extra days to do that. It would be nice to see the final results from the package I had gone through so much to ensure the safe delivery of. "I'll stay and see what happens when you send the signal."

"It's ok for you to stick around. Since we are a growing community, you can't just hang out and mooch our supplies, though. We'll gladly feed you today for making the delivery, but you will be expected to do some work for a stay longer than that."

"I grew up on a family farm. I can do some work for you in one of your greenhouses if they can use my help."

"The greenhouses are a little short of knowledgeable staff. Anything you can do in there would be greatly appreciated."

I worked in a few greenhouses while the communications system finished its preparations for the lab's first broadcast to the Arks. During the morning hours, I helped a crew harvest crops in one greenhouse. That same afternoon, I helped another group fertilize the soil for some winter crops that were about to be planted. I was able to help them balance the mixture of the fertilizers to improve the yield of their crops. Even though those I was working with were aware I was waiting for the results of the laboratory's computations, I didn't reveal what those computations were for. There was no way for me to know which of the laborers I was working with might agree with the Professor's goals and which ones didn't.

My entire second day of greenhouse duty was maintenance work. Watering rows of plants, weeding plots, checking for disease and rot amongst the leaves. Fortunately the nature of the greenhouses themselves prevented a large number of potential insects from getting to the plants. It did, however, lend itself to a higher risk of fungus and unwanted molds developing in the rich soil.

One of the younger women I had been working with woke me early in the morning of my third day at the growing compound. She had a message for me from Professor Joe. The computers were done and they were ready to send a signal. I hurried to the laboratory and walked up to the front door. The sign that had been missing when I first arrived was now clearly displayed next to the door. This time it was unnecessary as I had been told the proper procedure for entering the building already. I entered and went directly to Professor Joe's lab. He was there with two other men in lab coats.

"Welcome, Cade. We are going to head to the communications room as soon as the last member of our group gets here. In the meantime, let me make some introductions. Gentlemen, this young man is Cade. He is the messenger that was kind enough to get the data we needed here undamaged."

Professor Joe gestured to a man that looked old enough to have helped built the Arks. He had a full beard and no hair on his head. "Cade, this is Fred. He is our astronomer. For the last two years he has been studying stellar physics to help us track the locations of the Arks."

The Professor then pointed out the much younger of the two men already in the room. He was only a couple years older than me. He had a full head of dirty blonde hair and a hint of red in his mustache. "The young man over there is our laser expert, Ricky. All of the equipment is older than he is, but he has shown a special knack for keeping it all functioning efficiently."

Ricky smiled at the mention of his skills. "Mostly it's just cleaning mirrors and reconnecting loose wires. It isn't nearly as hard to keep old parts running as it is to build them in the first place."

The four of us talked about simple things like the weather and the offered menu at recent meals for a short time before the door to the lab opened and the missing member of our group entered. It was a young woman with long black hair flowing down her back. She had an average build and smooth face. Her crystal blue eyes seemed to shine enough to light up the entire room. I had never seen anything so beautiful in my entire life. If this angel had appeared in my hometown, I might have reconsidered my plan to travel as a messenger and instead, stayed around to start a family with her.

Professor Joe's voice brought my attention back to this world. "Cade, this is Alana. She is my assistant. The two of us will be monitoring the signal data and keeping the computers running to intercept any replies from the Arks."

Alana faced me and extended her hand. I grasped it and gave her a gentle handshake as she spoke. "Thank you, Cade, for bringing us that flash drive in such a timely manner. You don't know how fortunate your timing was. If you had come months earlier or later our alignment would have only allowed us to contact a couple of Arks. Where we are now will allow us to reach almost half of the Arks according to their planned courses and our calculations. The only question now is whether or not they are listening."

Professor Joe smiled a grin that stretched across his entire face as he reached out his arms to encompass all of us to guide us to the door out of the laboratory. "Let's all head to the communications room and see what we shall see."

We walked down an empty hall of the building. The other three men led the way as I walked behind them next to Alana. I didn't say anything to her, I just enjoyed being near enough to her that she was aware of my presence and I was aware of hers. As attractive as I found her, I didn't want to press myself onto her socially until we all knew if we were going to be celebrating their efforts or mourning time wasted.

Professor Joe led us around a corner of the hall and to a pair of double doors, which opened into a room full of electronic equipment and control consoles. At least three monitors were hung on each wall. The monitors displayed everything from star fields to power levels and frequencies. The equipment was all actively running. Strings of numbers were scrolling across screens. Points were flashing with identifying flags on them. Somewhere amongst all these indicators, lights, and knobs was the technology and instruments to talk to the Arks and the rest of humanity.

Joe and Alana each sat down at a terminal. Joe started typing feverishly. The words of a message appeared on the screen before him. Alana was making minute adjustments on her terminal. She spoke to us without taking her eyes off the screen before her.

"Thanks to Fred's calculations, we have located the general area of the first Ark we want to contact." She spoke with an accent that sounded strange to my ear. It was as though English wasn't her native tongue, but she had mastered it with much experience. "They aren't the closest, but we do have the clearest view of them once I fine tune this and locate their exact position."

Joe finished typing and made a swiping gesture across his screen. The text of his message slipped away and across the room to a screen next to Alana. "I have composed a message that lets them know we are alive and that nothing happened. There are also instructions for contacting us in return. It has been encoded for the laser and is ready to be sent."

"We tested our broadcast and reception equipment a few days ago with a signal to a relay station built on the moon. We just sent a simple message with instructions for it to be sent back to us. Everything worked perfectly for that short broadcast distance," Ricky said while Alana seemed to locate what she was looking for. Her screen zoomed in and one of the small points of light on it appeared to be moving slowly in relation to the others.

Some excitement crept into Alana's voice. "I have Ark #6, the Enterprise, located. They are close to where Fred calculated them to be. Since the pulse laser signal travels at the speed of light, the message should reach them in about 30 hours."

Alana entered a few commands on her terminal and reached to press a large green button. Her hand paused hovering over the button. She turned to look at the small group waiting anxiously behind her. "We have all worked so hard to be able to send this message. It seems selfish for me to take the privilege of sending the first message for myself. Why don't you guys come here and help me?"

I watched with a big grin as the others in the room walked over to Alana and placed their hands on hers. Professor Joe looked at me and nodded his head. "Cade, you might not have worked on any of the equipment here, but your contribution was very important. If you hadn't worked so hard to bring us the flash drive with the codes and calculations we needed, this wouldn't be possible at all. Please come join us."

I walked to the console and placed my hand on the stack that was already hovering over the green button set to activate the transmission. At a signal from Professor Joe we all pressed down on the button. The button sent a signal to the computers with the encoded message stored in their drives. The data of the message traveled through electronic passages to the laser broadcasting apparatus. The laser invisibly pulsed into the depths of space with words from one segment of humanity to another. It all happened in an anticlimactic silence for those of us in the room with our hands piled on the green transmission button.

Our hands separated and we all stepped back from the console. It was going to be a two and a half day wait for the automatic response that our signal had been received. A response would take longer as those on the Ark considered the message and its ramifications. It would also take some time for them to compose and encode a response. There were enough greenhouse crops ready to be harvested that I could wait until the automated response was received. There was nothing more to keep me from returning to my chosen profession of carrying messages after that.

I was busy enough in the greenhouses over the next two days that I completely lost track of how much time had passed. I didn't see anyone else from the communication room the entire time. It was during a communal dinner that Alana came and sat next to me. She waited until most of the seats around us emptied before speaking to me. Even then, she whispered so that only I could hear her. Her proximity and the warm breath against my skin were a little distracting. It was slightly difficult for me to focus on the words she was saying.

"While you were playing in the dirt, the rest of us have been monitoring the equipment and calculating the positions of other Arks. The automatic reply to our signal should be picked up in about 30 minutes. I am officially inviting you to join us for some celebrating once we have confirmation."

I nodded and the two of us quickly finished our meals. We got up together and returned our soiled dishes to the kitchen area. As we moved, I was infected by Alana's enthusiasm and energy. We quickly walked in step from the dining room and away from those still eating. Our excitement and synchronization might have led an unknowing observer to think we were in a hurry for a private, intimate activity instead of watching monitors for a signal sent by a computer hundreds of thousands of miles away.

We reached the communications center with seconds to spare. As we caught our breath, the computer console Fred was sitting at began to beep. The computers began to whir quietly as the laser transceiver collected the pulses of light and began to translate them into a message. The text began to appear on the screen. The letters formed words at a speed faster than anyone in the room could have typed.

"Message received. Proper personnel contacted. Expect initial reply shortly. Secondary reply will follow. No reply to this message expected." The words stopped appearing and we read them over repeatedly.

We all looked at each other. We had successfully contacted one of the Arks. At least one portion of humanity still existed in deep space. They now knew we were still alive and capable of communicating. Between the relief that the system worked, excitement at being able to send messages to the Arks, and a nervousness regarding what this truly meant for the people that still resided on Earth, none of us really knew how to react.

Grinning from ear to ear, his eyes shining brighter than the sun, Joe looked each of us in the eye. "I have a little something stashed away for this very occasion. It's been tucked away since this facility was fully staffed during the building of the Arks. I can't think of a better reason to pop it open than what is displayed on the screen right now. Would each of you like to help me in a little celebrating?"

After a chorus of agreement, Professor Joe reached behind one of the console cooling units and pulled a large bottle from it. The large wine bottle was coated in a layer of dust. The only places the green glass could be clearly seen were where Joe had gripped the bottle. It wasn't as ceremonial as the occasion called for, but Fred produced a set of coffee mugs for us to toast with. The five of us sipped from our mugs until the bottle was empty. As the other three huddled over the monitor displaying the Ark's automated response, Alana grabbed my hand and gave me an inviting nod towards the door of the lab. The amount of wine I had consumed wasn't enough to get me drunk. It was, however, allowing me to feel agreeable to Alana's implied invitation.

She led me to a side hallway. We entered a large office with a soft looking couch against one wall. She released my hand in order to start removing her meager clothes. I followed suit. We were both in our underclothes as I wrap my arms around her body and start kissing her. As one form, our two bodies fell onto the couch. I let the passion of the situation flow over me before my mind had a chance to intervene.

Our bodies moved and intertwined for an unknown amount of time. We collapsed sated and satisfied. Our arms and legs twisted around each other enough that it was difficult to tell which limb belonged to which body. Sleep came quickly to both of us despite the fact the couch wasn't built for two. I awoke some time later, alone and covered by a blanket that had been draped across the back of the couch earlier.

I gathered my clothes and quietly got dressed. I didn't know what time Alana left or whether she would be returning. The emptiness in my stomach told me it was time for some breakfast and I couldn't wait around long to find out if I would be eating with a companion this morning. I walked out of the office door and turned just in time to see Alana racing around the corner of the hallway towards me. Her face was alight with joy and excitement.

She spoke to me so quickly it took me an extra second to mentally translate the importance of what she had said. "We got a full response from the Ark. It is downloading now and the computers should be ready to play it just as we get back to the lab."

Alana grabbed my hand and practically dragged me back down the halls of the building to the computer room. I had just enough time to catch my breath after the unexpected sprint as the computer beeped to confirm that it had finished converting the signal from raw data to something we could hear.

The voice that emerged from the speakers was strong and experienced with only a slight tinniness after traveling such a vast distance. "Greetings to Earth from Captain Kirk Johnson of the Enterprise. We are all so very excited to hear from you. An impromptu holiday has been declared and will probably become an annual event.

"We have been maintaining contact and exchanging information with the Arks TARDIS and Good Ship Lollipop. Already the news of your continued survival had been relayed to those two Arks. They will be transmitting their own signals to you in due time.

"Despite our elation at knowing Mother Earth is still properly spinning, we have decided to continue on to our planned settlement. We dare not try to predict how the people of the other Arks will decide amongst themselves. It is our understanding that not all Arks were lucky enough to prosper as we have. Rumor floating between the stars is that there were a couple that failed entirely and nobody is still alive as the ghost ships now drift along.

"Once again, we are excited to hear from you and look forward to maintaining contact. Individual requests from residents and crew for information about the status of specific people left behind will be coming in the next week."

We had all stood in silence as the message played through. After the captain's voice faded from the speakers, we all remained quiet for a minute. The only sounds in the room were the computers processing data and the soft sounds of us barely breathing.

"Woooohoooo! Yes! Alright!" Ricky's sudden cheers made the rest of us jump a little. It also triggered cheers from the rest of us. Everyone was excited as we exchanged handshakes and pats on the back. Alana gave everyone a friendly hug and kiss on the cheek. She hugged me last and the kiss was not on the cheek and a lot friendlier than the one she had given the others.

Since we had consumed all the wine last night, Fred offered to go get another bottle from his private stash. Professor Joe decided to delay any further celebrations. "While that is a good idea, Fred, we have more work to do today contacting the other Arks. We will celebrate tonight after we locate the Arks and transmit the message to them.

Joe and Alana began reprogramming the message for each Ark while Fred and Ricky calculated locations and required signal strengths. While the others worked at their terminals, I left the laboratory building and went to collect some lunch for the others. I was certain their work would keep them occupied into the evening.

On the way back to the lab with some sandwiches, I decided it was time for me to move on. There were many reasons for me to remain here. I could help them with their greenhouses and considerably boost their yields. I would have to admit the social interactions with Professor Joe and the others was a nice break from the relative isolation of traveling the open roads. The chance of more private evenings with Alana was also rather tempting. However, there were more messages out there that needed delivering and many more sights for me to see and towns to visit. I had made my mind up to be a messenger and provide a valuable communication service to the scattered communities that remained. I may return to Redding some day and settle down. My time here would always be on my mind as I biked my way back and forth across the continent.

While I would keep quiet about Professor Joe and his people contacting the Arks, I would certainly keep my eyes open for anything else that those living amongst the stars might like to know. While I had no immediate plans to return to my hometown, I would definitely let the lab there know of the success in Redding that was aided by the package they gave me to deliver if I ended up there again.

I placed the sandwiches on an unused desk where they would easily be seen without interrupting anyone's work. I walked out of the lab and closed the door with a heightened sense of accomplishment accompanied by a hint of regret for leaving without saying farewell.

I had utilized more of the northern routes and highways on my way here. It might be nice to see some sights along the southern sections of the country. Even though I didn't have a specific destination in mind, the area around Florida had always looked nice in the pictures I had seen. My dad had told me about a launch center there that had been used even before the Exodus. If there happened to be a lab there similar to this one, I could take information I discovered on my journey there to be relayed to the Arks via whatever electronic mail system they had in place.

I felt anew that my journey was just beginning and it was a good feeling.

ACKNOWLEDGEMENTS

I want to thank my family for their patience with me while working this book. They put up with me not being there even when I was sitting right there in my chair.

I also wish to thank Julie and the other wonderful folks at Amazing Things Press for taking a chance on me and my tale.

Last, and certainly not least, I wish to thank you, the reader. You decided to explore this world I created. That is what makes this worthwhile.

A MESSAGE FROM THE AUTHOR:

Thank you for taking the time to read my book. I hope you enjoyed reading it as much as I did writing it. I would be honored if you would consider leaving a review for it on *Amazon*.

ABOUT THE AUTHOR:

Robert Christiansen was born in Las Vegas in 1979. At the age of 3 his family moved to the small town of Pahrump. He then spent most of the next two decades enjoying the view of the stars from the desert floor. He now lives north of Kansas City, Missouri with his wife and four energy-filled sons. Robert enjoys science fiction from multiple generations in all forms of media. He consumes books by Arthur C Clarke, Ray Bradbury, and Douglas Adams, savors radio shows Dimension X and Alien Worlds, and gets excited about television shows like Doctor Who, Firefly, and Dark Matters.

Find out more about Robert and his books at www.authorrobertchristiansen.weebly.com.

Check out these books from
Amazing Things Press

Keeper of the Mountain by Nshan Erganian

Rare Blood Sect by Robert L. Justus

Survival In the Kitchen by Sharon Boyle

Stop Beating the Dead Horse by Julie L. Casey

In Daddy's Hands by Julie L. Casey

MariKay's Rainbow by Marilyn Weimer

Convolutions by Vashti Daise

Seeking the Green Flash by Lanny Daise

Thought Control by Robert L. Justus

Tales From Beneath the Crypt by Megan Marie

Fun Activities to Help Little Ones Talk by Kathy Blair

Bighorn by James Ozenberger